Praise for Niqui Stanhope and her Novels

CHANGING THE RULES

"Romance with a hip attitude . . . steamy sexual tension and exuberant energy."
—*Publishers Weekly*

"In this funny, sexy, very contemporary romantic comedy, the rules ultimately bend nicely with satisfactory results for all concerned. This lively, sassy romp has appeal far beyond the targeted African American readership."
—*Library Journal*

"Stanhope writes with humor and compassion about young black professionals and their quest for true love."
—*Romantic Times*

"The romance is appealing, as fans will like the antics of the lead duo, particularly Marcel."
—*Midwest Book Review*

SWEET TEMPTATION

"Readers will fall in love."
—*Romantic Times*

MADE FOR EACH OTHER

"Niqui Stanhope has written a riveting story that pulls the reader along on a tide of sensuality, lush scenery, and unfor-gettable romance."

DISTANT MEMORIES

"*Distant Memories* is a taut, e̶x̶ ̶ showcases Ms. Stanhope's unique literary talents . . . the story is a 'must-read.'"
—*Romantic Times*

St. Martin's Paperbacks Titles
By Niqui Stanhope

Changing the Rules

Whatever Lola Wants

Whatever Lola Wants

Niqui Stanhope

St. Martin's Paperbacks

WHATEVER LOLA WANTS

Copyright © 2004 by Niqui Stanhope.

ISBN: 0-312-98624-6
EAN: 80312-98624-7

Printed in the United States of America

St. Martin's Paperbacks edition / September 2004

St. Martin's Paperbacks are published by St. Martin's Press, 175 Fifth Avenue, New York, NY 10010.

10 9 8 7 6 5 4 3 2 1

For all of the divas out there! I hope you enjoy Lola!
And, especially for: Noma

Prologue

Lola St. James sat behind her large oak desk, an expression of triumph in her eyes. It had taken her a good long while to arrange it, but now here he was, sitting right across from her. She had contacted him the week before and had arranged this meeting. She had told him that she wanted the grounds of her sprawling estate completely remodeled, with lots of bushes, trees, benches, artificial ponds. Whatever she'd been able to think of, she had thrown in. But what he didn't know was that landscaping was probably the furthest thing from her mind.

"I've heard you're good," she said now, and a sexy little smile lit the corners of her softly tilted almond eyes.

Chaz Kelly chuckled in a completely masculine manner and agreed in a warm baritone, "It's been said that I'm one of the best in the D.C. area." He dragged a straight-backed chair toward him with the yank of a foot, spun it so that his arms could rest along the smooth high back, and sat. "But it depends on what exactly you have in mind."

Laughter bubbled for a minute in Lola's chest, and she did her best to keep her amusement from showing. Good Lord almighty. He didn't recognize her. He really had no idea at all who she was. Well, he couldn't be blamed. The last time he had seen her, she had been a short and fat little girl called Sadie Green, with round pumpkin cheeks, an explosion of pimples, and thick, ugly braces. Now she had a long, lean body, a hard, flat stomach, sculpted cheekbones, smooth, unblemished skin. Now she called herself by her middle name, Lola—a name that better suited the woman she was today.

Her lips blossomed into a perky smile as the thought of it all shimmered in her eyes. It was completely all right, though. Completely all right. He would never forget her again . . . after she was through with him. If she ever got through with him.

She leaned forward to pick up the neatly typewritten contract and allowed him a glimpse of fragrant currant brown bosom.

"This," she said, in dulcet tones, "is something that I always have my employees sign." She waved a beautifully manicured hand. "It's just your standard boilerplate legalese. Here. Read it over, and let me know what you think." She gave him a wide smile. "There are a few other things I'll ask that you agree to in good faith once we get the contract out of the way. A few things that I absolutely insist upon. But I'm getting ahead of myself."

Chaz reached for the document, and Lola eyed him in a feline manner. Lord, but if he wasn't still one of the most gorgeous men she had ever laid eyes on. Over six feet tall. Smooth milk chocolate skin, short-cropped hair. Broad shoulders, a trim waist, a good tight butt. Eyes that were so dark they appeared almost coal black. She pressed her tongue into the corner of her lips. Yes, he was still as sexy as she remembered. Lord, the things she was going to do to him once she got started. Things she had wanted to do since they had first met in high school. A reflective little smile bent the curve of her mouth. It had been a long while since she had let herself think of those early years. They had literally run into each other during her freshman year. She'd been walking between classrooms, hustling as fast as her chubby legs would take her. He had come pelting around a corner, had crashed into her and knocked her books flying. She had braced herself for the usual slew of fat jokes and had watched in stunned incomprehension when instead of taunting her, as was the usual custom, he had helped pick up her books. She had been stunned by his kindness and had rewarded him with a wide smile. He had returned it and had surprised her again by walking all the way to class with her. And, with that simple act, a friendship had been born. He had been a jock, well on his way to capturing the coveted captain-of-the-football-team spot, and yet he had wanted to spend time with her. Had been kind to her even when everyone else had laughed and made fun of her round physique and pimples. She had loved him for that and for so many other reasons. She still remembered with sharp clarity the afternoons he had spent in her cramped brick-faced apartment in downtown D.C., helping her with chores that her poor overworked mother had been too worn out to attend to. It had been during those times that Lola had prayed hard for a slim and beautiful body, one that he would find attractive. She had cut back on all of her favorite foods for months, but instead of losing the weight, she had piled on even more pounds than ever. Finally, she had just given up and prayed instead that he would be able to love her for her inner beauty.

By her junior year, she had been thoroughly convinced that not only was she in love with him, but that he was beginning to return the feeling also. She would follow him with longing eyes whenever he was around, much to the amusement of the other kids. But she hadn't cared much about what they thought. She loved Chaz, and she didn't care who knew it.

After school, she would go faithfully to sit in the stands to watch him play ball, and daydream, waiting for him to run across the field at the close of practice to ask, "How'd I do today, chubby cheeks? Think I'm ready for the NFL yet?" She remembered how badly he had wanted that.

Memory clouded her eyes. They had been so close in those days that she had just known that it was only a matter of time before he asked her to be his girlfriend. And she had waited with an impatient heart for him to make his move.

But everything had changed on the day that Veronica Simms had joined the senior class. And his betrayal had cut Lola deeply. It had been inconceivable at the time for her to think that he would actually prefer a beautiful face and a tight, curvaceous little body to her wit and obvious intelligence. But he had. He had.

Lola's eyes glittered with memory. Veronica Simms, the daughter of an up-and-coming sports agent. She had been taller than everyone else, prettier than everyone else, and Chaz had behaved like a total fool over her. All of a sudden, he no longer had the time for Lola. There were no more evenings spent planning what they would do after high school. No more quick talks between classes. And after football practice he had started walking home with Veronica instead of with her.

The intensity of the affair had taken Lola completely by surprise, and she had been forced to watch the unfolding drama from the sidelines. But she had prayed. Every night before going to bed she had said a prayer that he would come to his senses and realize that Veronica Simms was not the right girl for him. That she, Sadie Green, was.

And she had not believed that her prayers were not to be answered until the very day he had come to her little apartment to say good-bye. His words had hit her like heavy blows to the chest. And throughout his entire little speech she had held tightly to her tears. She had vowed that she would not cry as he told her that he was going off to California to college and was taking Veronica with him. She could still hear his voice: *"I know Veronica's the right girl for me, Sadie. You know how much I want to play in the NFL, right? Well, her father's got connections. He can make it happen. And besides, you know how important image is once you get to that level, don't you?"*

She had nodded dumbly even though at the time she hadn't a clue as to what he really meant. He had reached forward then to hug her and had pressed a kiss to her cheek and said, *"Veronica knows all about that world, Sadie. She's pretty. She'll fit in."*

Then he had twisted the knife with brutal intent

when finally he put Lola at arm's length and said, *"You've got to forget about me and go on with your life, chubby cheeks. You know I'm not the one for you. And you . . . you're not the one for me, either. And besides, just think about it: You really wouldn't like that rich world of celebrities and money anyway. It's just not right for you. You'd be lost. You're not a flashy kind of girl. What you need is a nice average kind of guy who'll appreciate you. Someday, you'll make some lucky guy a wonderful wife."*

He had gone on to tell her that he would be married as soon as he and Veronica got out to California. And then as Lola still stared up at him with dry unformed words in the back of her throat, he had bent his head to press one warm sweet kiss to her numb lips. And it was in that very instant that she had known for sure that she would never forgive him.

Lola blinked rapidly as the memories swarmed before her eyes. After all these years, it still hurt to remember. She had hated him fiercely for the first five years or so after high school. Then the hatred had turned to anger, and the anger to determination. All of her life she had been a fat little girl, but she had made a vow on that day that henceforth things would be different. She would make something of herself. She would change herself so completely that the next time he saw her . . .

"I'm sorry, what?"

His gravelly voice caused a skitter of warmth to run the length of her spine.

Chaz tapped a thick finger against the creamy yellow bond.

"There's something here I don't exactly understand."

Lola crossed her legs and said sweetly, "What is it?"

Smooth black eyes met hers across the short distance, and for the first time in years, Lola's heart gave an unsteady tremble. She was going to have to figure out really fast how exactly she was going to get this man between her thighs.

She reached a hand for the document and asked in a warm manner, "May I?"

Chapter One

Lola looked at the papers for a moment. "I think the wording in the contract is very clear," and she stood so that he could get a good look at her. She was a tall satin brown woman, a striking beauty with shoulder-length raven black hair, a curvy Coke bottle body, and fine Ethiopian features. Her legs were long, her thighs were thick, and her derriere was just large and rounded enough to send most red-blooded adult males into a serious case of conniptions. She had the look of a woman who was well used to getting exactly what she wanted. And, in most cases, she did.

She stood just a pace away from Chaz, a hand perched neatly against her right hip. Her eyes flickered over him in a quick little analytical sweep, and she noted with some amount of irritation that he didn't seem at all impressed by her body. Her lips tightened by just a bit. OK. Fine. So he wasn't going to be easy, but she had broken harder men than he. A little smile curved the corners of her mouth. She was going to make him want her. And not only that, but he was going to love every moment of it before she sent him packing.

Chaz cleared his throat and then said in an extremely pleasing baritone, "It says here," and he flipped a page with a thick finger, "that the compensation for completing this job is one million dollars? And there's also a discretionary bonus?"

Lola nodded and one of her eyebrows lifted. "Were you hoping for a little more than that?"

Chaz laughed. "More? No. I think the million will be sufficient."

Lola folded her arms. "Then what's the problem?"

He came to his feet, so that Lola was forced to look up at him.

"What kind of discretionary bonus are we talking about? I mean, is it a time-dependent kind of thing? You want this job done by a certain date and if I bring it in on schedule there's a little more cash involved?"

Lola met his eyes. "Actually, no. The bonus has nothing to do with how quickly you finish the job. It has to do with something else entirely."

She could see that she had captured his interest with that, and she gave him a deliberate moment to consider exactly what she might mean.

"I'm guessing that whatever it is, it's too far outside the letter of the law for you to include it in the contract."

Lola chuckled. Oh, it was going to be so much fun taking him down. What would he think? What would he really think about it if he knew that she, Lola St. James, was Sadie Green? The same fat little girl he had once referred to as "not flashy. Ordinary."

"You're right," she said. "I think you'll probably find my request a little, shall we say, unorthodox?"

"Well, as long as it doesn't involve anything illegal, I'm willing to at least listen to what you have to say."

"I'll give you an extra twenty thousand dollars if

during the completion of this project, you agree to put any possible marital plans that you might have on hold." She leaned forward. "I mean, I have no idea of what you might be doing in your personal life, of course, and really, when it comes right down to it, it's neither here nor there to me what you do. But what I do care about is the job, and the quality of work. And I've found that whenever there's a woman involved . . ." She let the rest of her sentence hang. It was a lie, of course. She did care very much about everything he did in his personal life. A long time ago she had had to stand by and watch another woman take him. But she wouldn't be standing on the sidelines this time. She, Lola St. James, was going to have him for as long as she liked. And judging by the way he looked in those tight jeans and white T-shirt, that might turn out to be a very long time.

Chaz looked at her for a long moment, and Lola waited, her face calm, cool. Whenever the need was there, she could play a mean hand of poker.

"You're serious about this," he finally said. "Twenty thousand dollars extra for not doing something that I had no plans to do in the first place?"

Lola released the breath she'd been holding. "Twenty thousand dollars extra. Call me eccentric. But those are my terms."

Chaz stretched his legs before him, and Lola's eyes followed the ripple of muscle in his thighs.

"I need the money. There's no question about that. But I'm not sure about this. It doesn't feel right, taking bonus money in this way."

Lola gritted her teeth. He had to agree to this. He

had to. She didn't want to have to divert her energies toward getting rid of another woman.

"I'm a rich woman. So don't concern yourself about the money. This bonus is my personal stipulation. Think about it before you decide to turn it down. You can still do a few things these days with twenty thousand dollars."

Chaz drew his feet in, stood. "OK. I'll think about everything you've said. I'll let you know tomorrow, if that's OK with you? I'd like my lawyer to have a look at . . . " And he began to move toward the door to the sleek oak-paneled office.

"You don't have a steady woman, do you?" Lola stopped his progress with a deceptively soft query.

Chaz turned. "What?"

"She's not part of the deal, even if you do."

The doorway leading to the short flight of stone stairs was partially open, and hot sunshine cast a puddle of bright light on the wooden floor.

"Excuse me?"

And for the first time in their hour-long meeting Lola heard the hint of steel in his voice.

"You can't move any of your female friends in here. Onto the property, I mean. The guesthouse is really only properly equipped for a bachelor. A woman wouldn't be happy there. Besides, as I said before, I don't want anything to distract you from your work." She took a breath and waited half a beat to see how this new stipulation struck him. Thus far he had weathered the entire affair with remarkable equanimity. But this, this would be another matter entirely, and hence the reason she had saved it for the very end.

"I don't understand you."

"It's simple. What I'm saying is whatever you do off the property is your own business, but I won't agree to you having women living here with you. And I'm not flexible at all about that." Now there was steel in *her* voice.

Their eyes did battle for a moment, and then Chaz said in a hard, flat voice, "Not that it's any of your business either way. But I'm trying to raise my son up with the right moral values . . . and living together with a woman I'm not married to is not one that I want to pass along to him."

Lola blinked rapidly. So did that mean he didn't have a girlfriend? Or that he just didn't let her stay overnight with him? Lord, but he was a slippery talker.

"You have a son?" she asked now with what she hoped was the adequate amount of surprise in her voice. Of course it hadn't been anything new to hear him say he did. She had known about the boy all along. But Chaz couldn't know that.

Chaz allowed the half-open door to rest against the curve of his boot, and he said in a manner that almost brought a flush of embarrassment to Lola's cheeks, "Yes, I do. And I hope one of your requirements won't be that I can't bring him along with me. Because if that's the case, I'll tell you now that—"

"No, no, no," Lola interrupted him hastily. "Of course you can bring your child along with you. I'm not heartless, you know . . . regardless of what you might have heard."

"Right," Chaz said, and the tone in his voice made Lola tighten her lips. It didn't matter if every other man in the world thought of her as a cold, ruthless barracuda. She didn't want this one to. She didn't want Chaz Kelly to think so, too.

"I think you'll find, once you start working with me, that I'm a very reasonable and understanding woman."

He nodded at her and said in a manner that set Lola's nerves on edge, "Yes. I'm sure I will. Well, see you tomorrow."

From the floor-to-ceiling plate-glass windows Lola followed him with thoughtful eyes as he walked down the stone stairs and across the well-kept green lawns. *Tomorrow. Yes. Everything would begin tomorrow.*

Chapter Two

Chaz Kelly got into his ten-year-old Toyota truck and closed the door. Lord, if that hadn't been a meeting for the record books. When he had received the summons from Lola St. James's office, he had been of two minds whether to accept the offer of a meeting. But of late his landscaping and pool design business had really begun to struggle. Most months he barely managed to pay the skeleton crew of employees who worked for him. In fact, things had gotten so very bad in the last six months that he had seriously considered closing shop altogether.

He reversed down the curved pink gravel drive. This wasn't supposed to be his life. If the fates had been fair at all, he would be playing pro ball right now and living the good life out in California. That had been how he had planned his life. Since high school he had had dreams of playing for the NFL. And he had had the talent to do it, too. He had played ball on a full scholarship at USC and had been a first-round draft pick with the 49ers in his junior year. He had received a thick eight-figure contract for five years. And the sweet life had swept him up. He had married Veronica Simms, a girl he'd met in high school, bought a big house out in the Bay Area, and settled in to live long and hard, doing all of the things that young sports celebrities with way too much money tend to do. But just when everything seemed to be going his way, life had gone and changed the program on him. On a perfectly simple pass, on a perfectly ordinary day, he had slipped, fallen, severely injured his knee, and ended his NFL career. Looking back on it now, he still couldn't understand how the accident had happened. It had taken him many years to come to grips with the reality that the life he had planned and worked so hard for was no more. His wife, who had grown quite accustomed to a certain standard of living, a certain way of life, had realized, too, that the life they had been living was no more. And very shortly after he received the lump sum settlement on his five-year contract, she had informed him that she was leaving him for another NFL player. Their son, Jamie, was just a few months old at the time.

Chaz shifted gears with some difficulty, checked his rearview mirror, and then pulled onto the black tar street. Life, frankly, had been much less than fair to him. But he wasn't complaining. In the big scheme of things, it really could have been much worse. Much worse. At least he still had his health. He was thirty-six years old. He had a ten-year-old son who was the spitting image of him at that age and he had an ordinary relationship with the kind of woman who would probably be a good wife for him and a decent mother to his son. Admittedly, there was no great passion between them. But they were both beyond that silly stage where they believed in sparks, chemistry, and true love anyway. And, frankly, if love hadn't bitten by the grand old age of thirty-six, it was highly unlikely that it was ever going to bite. That was the pure and simple truth of it.

As a teenager tore by on a motorcycle Chaz shrugged and glanced into his side-view mirror. He didn't have the time for all of that foolishness anyway. He was a grown man with the problems and concerns of a grown man. So now he had the chance to make an amazing chunk of money over the next twelve months and to make some very valuable connections, too, in the bargain. It was a well-known fact in certain circles that if Lola St. James recommended you on a job, it was as good as yours. And the good Lord knew that Chaz needed more than a few good solid jobs. He was currently living in a tiny utility apartment in the Washington, D.C., metro area. A place that was no good at all to raise a young boy. A fond smile flickered across his face. It wasn't easy raising a child alone, but Jamie was a good kid, even though of late he had started giving Chaz a bit of trouble. It still amazed him that the boy was his. He shuddered whenever he thought back on his own childhood. At ten years old, he had been a little monster. The things he had gotten into at that age horrified him to even think about now. What he had needed, though, was a strong paternal hand. A father to straighten him out. But he had never known the man who had fathered him, and his mother, poor thing, had done the best she could with what she had. And raising a headstrong son all alone in Washington, D.C., hadn't been easy.

He slowed the flatbed truck as he approached an intersection. This was one of the ways he picked up a lot of business. Many days he drove around wealthy neighborhoods in the Maryland and Virginia areas just looking at houses. If he saw anything promising, he would pull over to the curb, write down the location of the house, and then stick a business card and brochure in the mailbox. Very often, the owner ended up calling. But it was a slow process, and with a growing boy and Chaz's small staff to support, it was hard. Even after ten years of steady struggle to stay afloat, it still wasn't substantially easier than when he had first gotten into the business. But maybe things were about to change.

A rambling Victorian house came into view as he rounded a thickly treed corner, and Chaz slowed the truck so that he could take a good look at it. His keen eye took in the neatly manicured green lawns, the smooth stone fountains spouting crystal clear water, the symmetrically pruned bushes. It was a beautiful property; there was no question about that. But the grounds needed a bit of landscaping help.

He pulled over to the curb, cut the engine, and climbed out. He stuffed some promotional material into the fancy mailbox and then hopped back into the truck. The engine started with a surprised cough, and Chaz noted with a frown that his final stack of brochures was beginning to run a bit thin. He wiped a calloused hand across his jaw. Lord almighty, it was so hard to succeed as a small businessman these days. It was almost as though the system was set up to ensure failure. He couldn't get the kind of loan that he needed because he didn't have enough collateral. And he couldn't get enough collateral because he couldn't get himself a decent loan. A wry expression pulled at the corner of his mouth. He would have to accept Lola St. James's offer, bizarre stipulations and all. As far as he could see, he really didn't have a choice. His little ploy about wanting to have his lawyer look over the contract she had presented him with had been nothing more than a stalling technique. He couldn't afford to hire a lawyer even if his life depended on it. He routinely handled his own contracts. It wasn't always the wisest thing to do, but it was something that he had had to do. And, over the years, he had become a pro of sorts. He knew what kinds of things to look for. And he could spot a potential rip-off as fast as most trained lawyers could.

He shifted gears, grimacing at the sound his gear-box made.

Of course he would accept the offer, there was no other way that he could manage to keep body and soul together. So the fact that she appeared to have some sort of a personal interest in him was an unwelcome little problem that he would just have to deal with. He knew her by reputation of course. Most people in the business did. She was a well-known player. A ruthless, cold-hearted iron woman whose climb to the top of the construction world had been nothing short of legendary. She had stepped on, outwitted, and outmaneuvered some of the best people in the business. It was even rumored that she had ties to organized crime (which he was sure was just a rumor). But whatever dirty deals she had made to get to where she was today, they had all been nicely sanitized away by her high-priced team of Ivy League lawyers. Now she was squeaky clean and perfectly respectable. Just last week her photograph had appeared in one of the local scandal sheets. Chaz had noticed the screaming headline while standing in line at the checkout counter: "LOCAL SENATOR TO WED CONSTRUCTION QUEEN." And it had all made perfect sense to him. People who sought power were attracted to power. Lola St. James had gotten herself all the money; now she was going for influence, respectability. A senator's wife. What could be better than that?

His eyes narrowed against the noonday sun as the thought struck him. So what in the name of heaven did she want with him? Chaz Kelly. A washed-up former NFL player who was just managing to scrape out a living for himself? No, her less than subtle flirting had not been lost on him. They had never met before; of that he was completely certain. So what was her particular interest in him? It was all very puzzling.

His brow rippled. Of course there was another possibility. Maybe the senator was no good in the sack. Chaz wasn't unaware that women far and wide found him attractive. He had never had any trouble at all in that department. But if that was her intention, she was certainly barking up the wrong tree. Women like Lola St. James were trouble with a capital *T*.

And he wasn't naïve enough or immodest enough to believe that her obvious interest in him was based on the fact that she found him irresistible. She could get herself any man she wanted. He knew that. And if the rumors were only 50 percent accurate, it meant that she had made her way through a good number of men already.

He paused at the final intersection and then headed for the interstate highway, a thoughtful expression on his face. In his younger years, when he was into women like her, he might have chased a Lola St. James and had fun doing it, too. He was a man, after all, and he loved a beautiful woman as much as the next guy. But these days he had more important things on his mind, and he had neither the time nor the desire to play with a female barracuda. What he needed was a mother for his son. Someone who would have his back. Someone who could match him in and out of bed. What he needed was a lover. A wife. Not someone like Lola St. James. *Not* someone like Lola St. James. . . .

Chapter Three

Lola watched the first truck and then the second and third drive up the gravel drive. She hadn't been this excited in years. She had moved heaven and earth to get him here, and now, now he was right under her nose, exactly where she had always wanted him. Hard work really did pay off. It had taken a good deal of planning to bring the entire thing about, but she had done it. She had done it. And now she was going to enjoy him like she had never enjoyed another man before. Chaz Kelly. Jesus, how she had loved him once. He had never had any idea of how very deep her feelings for him had been. And back then, it hadn't been puppy love, either. It had never ever been puppy love. It had been real. As real as any love that had ever existed.

The cordless phone on her desk rang melodiously, and she walked across to utter a vaguely irritated, "Hello?"

Camille Roberts said a cheerful, "Hello yourself. What're you doing answering your phone? I thought you'd be all over that man by now. Or hasn't he shown up yet?"

The voice on the other end of the line made Lola smile. "He's here all right. I'm just giving him a little time to settle in. I don't want to seem too anxious again. You know what I . . . " But the rest of her sentence tapered off as the face of a little boy appeared in the large old-fashioned glass window.

"Hold on a second, girl," she said. "Seems like his little boy's come to pay me a visit. Don't go away." She rested the portable phone on the desk and went across to the window. She unlatched one section of the beautifully fashioned glass and looked out.

"Well, hello there," she said.

The little boy was standing ankle deep in a flower bed and asked with puzzlement in his voice, "Do you live here, too?"

Lola smiled at him. "Uhm-hmm. This is my house. And, let me guess, you must be Jamie. Am I right?"

Dark intelligent eyes met hers and the little brow furrowed. "Did my dad tell you about me?"

Lola leaned both elbows on the whitewashed windowsill. He was a handsome little boy. Smooth milk chocolate skin. Neatly cropped hair, coat black eyes. Some day, he would be a beauty.

The child smiled and said, "I like climbing trees."

Lola chuckled. "You do?"

"Yeah," the little boy said. "But we live in Washington, D.C., so I don't get to do it a whole lot."

"Well, we've got a few trees here, but you're not to climb any of them until your father says it's OK. Deal?"

"OK," Jamie agreed. "But what can I do then?"

Lola straightened away from the sill. Keeping a ten-year-old entertained was not her area of expertise, but he seemed like a sweet boy. "How about if you go explore the property? There are lots of squirrels and a few rabbits around."

"Really?" The child's face lit up. "And I can play with them?"

A smile curled the corners of Lola's mouth. "If you can catch them. They're pretty quick, you know."

The boy beamed at her. "Don't worry. I can catch them. See ya." And before Lola could say much of anything else, he was gone.

She closed the window, locked it, and then picked up the phone.

"You still there?"

"I was just about to hang up," Camille said. "So, what's the son like?"

Lola sat in the comfortable black leather chair and propped her feet on the smooth oak desk.

"He seems sweet. He's got personality. And not a shy bone in him anywhere."

They spoke for a while about Jamie, until Camille asked with a wicked note in her voice, "So, what're you going to do if some sexy chick comes calling as soon as Big Daddy's settled?"

Lola laughed softly and ran a hand over a smoothly curvaceous hip. "Please, do you really think I'd let any woman take him now that he's right under my nose? Besides, he doesn't have a girlfriend."

Camille's voice was slightly incredulous: "He told you that?"

"Not in so many words, of course. But he turned down my bonus incentive and told me that he couldn't take money from me when he wasn't planning on get-

ting married anytime soon. So that means he doesn't
have anyone too serious. Right?"

A knock on the oak-paneled door made her say hur-
riedly, "Look, I've gotta go. But come over for dinner
tonight, OK?"

She pressed the red button on the phone and then
called, "Come in!"

Her housekeeper, Annie, bustled in, her face
wreathed in smiles. She knew all about Lola and Chaz,
and she was as pleased as punch that he was finally
here.

"The trucks are here," she said beaming, and she
came forward to envelop Lola in a warm hug.

Lola returned the embrace for a minute and then
pulled away to say, "So, have you seen him?"

The matronly woman nodded and said happily,
"He's helping unpack the first truck."

Lola smoothed the skirt of her summer dress in a little unconscious motion. "Should I go over and offer to
help? You know how helpless men are about knowing
where to put things in a new house."

Annie Lewis tapped a thoughtful finger against the
round of her chin.

"No, don't do that. Give him some time." Her eyes
gleamed in sudden thought. "In an hour or two, they'll
both be hungry and I'll invite him and his little boy
over for some sandwiches and cake. You'll all have a
nice meal out on the patio."

"I'm not that great around children," Lola admitted.
"It's just that I've never really been around them before. But I do like them."

Annie gave her an encouraging pat on the arm.

"I know you do, Lola sweetheart. I know the sweet, kind, loving woman that you are. But you've got to show Chaz what I already know. Show him your true self. I don't want to see any of this hard-nosed businesswoman business when he's around. OK?"

Lola pressed her lips closed. She couldn't tell darling Annie that her original plan had just been to make Chaz fall for her, and then walk right out of his life. When she actually articulated it in that way, the whole thing seemed positively stupid, juvenile at best, and Annie wouldn't have approved.

Then, at Lola's expression, Annie shook her head and said laughingly, "If you can conquer the business world, you can have lunch with one man and one little boy."

"Jamie!" Chaz shouted. He wiped a hand across his brow and muttered, "Now where can that boy have gone to?" He cast a quick eye about and then said to one of the men helping him unload the truck, "Have you seen my boy?"

"He was just here," the other man said. "You want me to go find him?"

"No," Chaz said, and he heaved a large chest of drawers to the ground. "He's probably off somewhere reading." And there was a note of pride in his voice. Jamie was way above his grade level in both English and Math. Sometimes it was all Chaz could do to tear him away from studying. He'd probably be a doctor or lawyer when he grew up.

A short distance away at the main house, Lola was

deep in her closet, going through the contents like a woman possessed. There was a pile of clothing in a jagged semicircle on the floor, and still she hunted while muttering, "No. No. Not right. Too short. Too tight. Wrong color. Just plain ugly. God, I just don't have anything, anything at all, to wear." Finally she emerged from the belly of the closet to bellow, "Annie, can you come a minute?"

When Annie appeared, Lola said with a note of desperation in her voice, "I can't find it. I thought I had something decent I could wear, but nothing works. I just don't have anything at all that looks good."

"Now, Sadie," the older woman began.

"It's Lola . . . God. Don't forget and call me Sadie in front of him. That would just be it. The whole thing would be ruined."

"OK, OK. Lola. You're getting yourself into a knot over something as simple as choosing clothes? What's the matter with you? Have you forgotten that you're Lola St. James? The human dynamo? The woman who can make big strong men cry?"

Lola sighed. "Business is different. I know how to handle men in that kind of situation when I'm being Lola . . . but this whole softer side of me thing, I know it's there, but I just haven't done it in a good long while. You know?"

"Wear this," Annie said, and she pulled a soft oversize T-shirt and a pair of jeans from where they hung.

Lola took the proffered items and held them up to the light.

"Do you think it's right? The jeans are pretty tight. Especially in the rear. And—"

"That's why you have the T-shirt, to cover all of that up. And don't think for a second that you have to look frumpy in order to show him you've got a softer side. You have to look attractive as well as capable if you want that man to notice you."

"You're sure the jeans do it, though?"

"Positive." The housekeeper nodded.

"Are the sandwiches and cake ready?"

"Just about. I'll go looking for the child as soon as you're ready. I saw him run into some bushes a little while ago."

Lola sucked in a breath. "Right. OK. I can do this."

Chapter Four

Annie Lewis pushed open the screen door to the patio and took a look about the rolling green lawns. She nodded her graying head, and there was a glint of satisfaction in her eyes. Yes, it was a beautiful place all right. Lola had done good. The world could think whatever they liked about Lola St. James, but she, Annie Lewis, knew the truth. She had been with Lola from the time her mother had passed. Had been there on the very night when the poor soul had slipped from this world into the next. Annie had made a promise on that night to take care of Sadie . . . of Lola, to make sure that she walked the right path in life. And over the years it had been a pleasure to do just that. The world thought Lola was hard and cold, but they didn't know her. They didn't understand where she had come from. They didn't know how difficult it had been. How at the tender age of seventeen she had been forced to become the breadwinner for the family. How she had had to take care of her mother when she had gotten sick and could no longer help herself. It had been a long, hard struggle for Lola, putting herself through college, working two jobs, and trying to establish herself in a traditionally male business. But somehow she had done it.

Annie blinked her eyes against a sudden misting of tears. And now that the child had finally decided to settle, Annie would move heaven and earth to help her get the man she said she wanted.

Annie walked out onto the beautifully cut stone stairs, shaded her eyes against the sinking sun, and called, "Hello? Little boy?"

Behind a thick clump of trees not too far off, Jamie paused to listen. The voice was one he didn't recognize, so after listening for a bit more he ignored it and went back to his fascinating new project.

He leaned back against the scaly trunk of a tree, shook a cigarette into the palm of his hand, and examined it. He put it in his mouth and rolled it from side to side. It had a weird smell, but his friend Jamal, who knew everything about everything, said that Jamie wouldn't be a man until he had had one of these. And he was a man, there was no question about that.

Jamie lit the cigarette, sucked in, gasped, and hacked.

Annie walked in the direction of the sound, her brows beginning to wrinkle into lines of concern. The poor child sounded as though he was coming down with a serious case of flu. Well, she would soon do something about that.

The housekeeper rounded the thicket of trees and then came to an abrupt halt. The saints be protected, the child didn't have the flu at all. The little truant was smoking. *Smoking.*

"Little boy," she began with a note of steel in her voice.

Jamie jumped as though he had just been touched by

a cattle prod. He removed the lit cigarette from between his lips and attempted to hide it behind his back.

"Who're . . . who're you?" he stuttered.

Annie drew in a breath, and her massive bosom heaved as she did so. She had raised four children, all grown men and women now, but these kids today, she would never understand them.

"Get to your feet, young man," she said, and she reached forward to help him do so. "What is that you have in your hand?"

The child pouted, gave her a baleful stare. "Nothing."

Annie's jaw set, and dangerous lights began to glint in her eyes.

"Nothing? What do you mean, nothing?"

Jamie glared back at her, his eyes slightly narrowed. And for an unconscious moment he imitated one of the mannerisms he'd seen his father use on difficult employees.

"I know who you are," he said after a stretch. "You're just the maid. And this isn't even your house. So you can't tell me what to do."

Annie nodded. "Oh? Is that right?" And she grabbed a hold of one of the boy's arms and yanked him toward her. "Listen to me, you little . . . monster. I will take a switch to your behind faster than you can say 'Daddy.' You understand me?" And she gave him a little shake to emphasize her point.

There was a momentary struggle as the little boy twisted and turned in her strong grip. When it became apparent that such an approach was futile, he let fly with a foot and connected solidly with Annie's shin.

The momentary shock of that loosened Annie's grip

on him, and Jamie twisted free and sprinted off in the direction of the small guesthouse.

The expression on Annie's face was thunderous as she strode back through the open French doors. Lola, who was halfway down the long, curving staircase dressed in the oversize white T-shirt and stonewashed jeans, said with a note of sudden alarm in her voice, "What? What's happened?"

Annie sucked in a breath, released it, and then gave herself a moment to settle into one of the overstuffed sofas. When she was completely calm, she said, "I'm gonna wear that little boy's behind *out*."

Lola's eyebrows arched. "Jamie?"

"Yes, Jamie. You know what that boy did?"

Lola came to sit beside her. "But he's supposed to be such a sweet little kid. Are you sure you didn't run into some other child?"

Annie gave her a speaking look, and Lola conceded with a half chuckle, "All right. All right. So what did he do?"

Chapter Five

Chaz rubbed a fond hand across his son's head. "So where did you disappear to earlier on?"

Jamie gave his father a wide-eyed smile. "Nowhere special. Just around. . . ."

Chaz picked up a brown carton, placed it on the kitchen table, and with quick hands began to unpack a stack of brightly colored ceramic plates. He walked across to one of the nicely finished cupboards and Jamie followed him over with a short pile of plates.

"We'll put these up here. Seem OK to you?" Chaz looked down at the boy.

"OK with me," Jamie said, and he handed his father the plates and then went back across to the table to collect some more.

Chaz carefully arranged the lower shelf and then moved to the one above. "Think you're going to like living here?"

Jamie passed him an assortment of chipped blue and green cups. "It's all right."

"You can still visit your friends in D.C. whenever you want to. You know that, right?"

"Uhm-hmm."

Chaz arranged the cups in a haphazard cluster.

"What's the name of that friend of yours? The one you met at the mall just the other day?"

"Jamal."

Chaz nodded. "Right. Jamal. Maybe you can have him up here for the weekend one of these weeks. Once we're settled in, of course."

Jamie's eyes brightened. "Really, Dad?"

"Of course you can, son. You know that—" He was interrupted by the pealing of the front doorbell.

Chaz glanced in the direction of the sound. "Now who could that be? Jamie, go see who it is. And don't just open the door. We still have to be safe out here," he said as the boy tore off toward the front door.

Lola stood back at the sound of locks turning. She was almost surprised at the butterflies in her stomach.

"Well, hello there," Lola said as the solid oak door inched open to reveal the wiry little boy with close-cropped hair and blacker-than-night eyes.

The intelligent eyes looked her over.

"You're the lady from the big house."

Lola tried a twenty-watt smile. "I'm glad you remember me, Jamie." The little tyke didn't look like a handful at all. Maybe Annie had just gotten her signals crossed. She was known to be a bit old-fashioned from time to time.

"Dad!" the boy bellowed. "It's the lady from the big house. Should I let her in?"

Chaz stepped down from the wooden stool. Christ almighty. What was she doing here? Was this the way things were going to be for the next year? His privacy was something that he valued very highly, and he didn't take kindly at all to having his space invaded without invitation. Sure she owned the house, but for the next twelve months this little place was his, and the sooner she realized it the better.

He came forward and greeted her with a professional tone in his voice. "Miss St. James. What a surprise to see you so soon. We're just getting ourselves moved in, as you can see." He gestured to the boxes scattered all across the floor.

A little shiver raised the baby fine hairs at the nape of her neck as Lola met his dark eyes. Yes, this was why she had never married. This was why she now held the advances of a senator at bay. This was why she was going to make this man her very own.

"I brought you some sandwiches and cake. My way of saying 'Welcome.' I've got some cheese here, cold cuts, roast beef, tuna. Do you like tuna, Jamie?" She turned her attention to the little boy who had been silent since he had summoned his father to the door.

She was rewarded with a beaming smile and a nod. "Yes, ma'am."

"Good," Lola said, and she headed into the belly of the house and made a beeline for the kitchen before Chaz could utter a single word of invitation.

"You can stop for a brief snack now. And then I'll help you straighten out these boxes. What you need is a woman's touch," she tossed over her shoulder. "But don't worry; we'll sort things out."

"Ah . . . Miss St. James," Chaz said, following rapidly in her wake. "Listen. . . ."

"Lola. I told you to call me Lola. Everyone does." She placed the plate in her hands onto the kitchen counter and then reached into an openmouthed box to retrieve a pair of potbellied glasses.

She placed these crisply on the counter and declared in a bright tone, "Lemonade. You need something to drink. I'll have my housekeeper bring us some." She unsnapped her cell phone from her waistband and began to dial.

"Lola," Chaz tried again. "There's no need to bother yourself. We'll be just—"

"It's no bother," she said, waving away his protests with a little sweep of her hand. "You have to eat, don't you? And little Jamie here looks as though he might eat a horse. You're hungry, aren't you, sweetheart?"

Jamie looked at his father's face and then back at her.

"No, ma'am. I'm not that hungry."

Lola spoke rapidly into the phone and then closed it with a snap.

"Come on," she said to Chaz. "Have a little food. You can go right back to unpacking once you're done. You have to admit, what I've got here is healthier than pizza."

A reluctant smile curved a corner of Chaz's mouth. "I guess it must be true, what they say about you."

Lola arched an eyebrow. "*They* say so many things. Which one are you talking about?"

Chaz pulled out a stool and gestured for her to have a seat.

"The part about you being a force of nature and never taking no for an answer."

Lola sat. "I believe in getting what I want."

Chaz held her gaze for an instant. "Is that right?"

Devilry glittered in Lola's eyes. "That's right."

"Well . . ." And he drummed the fingers of one hand in a brief staccato against the surface of the kitchen table.

"Jamie, go over to Miss St. James' house and help the lady who's bringing the lemonade across. What's her name?" He turned questioning eyes toward Lola.

"Annie Lewis," Lola said, "but Mrs. Lewis to you," and winked at Jamie. "Her husband died a while back."

Chaz nodded. "Help Mrs. Lewis so she doesn't have to walk all the way over here. OK?"

The boy nodded, reluctantly. "OK."

Once the front door had closed behind the little boy, Chaz leaned toward her.

"Look, Lola."

She lowered her voice to a deliberately seductive pitch.

"Yes, Chaz."

Already she could smell the smooth satin sheets, taste the flickering candlelight, see the tangled, sweaty limbs.

"I think before we go any further, we'd better establish a few ground rules."

Lola shrugged. "OK. Rules are often good things to have." Plans were also good and she had more than a few of her own. But hers involved keeping him up all night and taking him places that even he, man of the world that he was, had never been. "Let's hear it."

Chaz nodded. "First off, I think with me living on the property for the next little while, there should be some boundaries. I don't know how you feel about kids—"

"Oh, I love kids," Lola said, "so if you're concerned about Jamie, don't be."

"That's good to know," Chaz said, and he gave a brief little smile that brought a surprising flush of blood to Lola's cheeks. "But the point I'm getting at is this: I'm your employee."

"Right," Lola said. "But what—"

"Let me finish. Since I'm working for *you*, and living in such close proximity to *you*, it wouldn't be wise if we allowed our daily situation to blur the lines that should exist between us. You understand what I mean?"

"Yes, I think I can see where you're going with this," Lola said, leaning forward so that her elegant nose was no more than an inch away from his. "But I think you're afraid."

Coal black eyes met hers and held. "What?"

She crossed her legs in a dainty little movement and leaned deliberately away from him.

"I think you're afraid of . . . me."

The serious expression on his face cracked at that, and Chaz threw back his head and guffawed. And the sound of it was so deep and so very pleasing that it drew an answering gamine grin to Lola's face.

"Well, I'm just trying to be honest," she said. "Most men are intimidated by me."

His eyes glinted with humor, and Lola experienced a pure burst of happiness. He no longer appeared so world-weary. For that brief moment of laughter, the lines of stress across his brow had smoothed. The tiredness about his eyes had lifted.

She sucked in a tiny breath. Lord, if he would only let her in.

"Let me put your mind at ease, Miss Lola St. James.

The woman hasn't been born yet who can get under my skin. I was merely suggesting that it might be a good idea to maintain a certain . . . Shall we say, professional distance."

"Do I have the power to force you to do anything you don't want to?"

He considered the question with half a smile beginning to twitch at the corners of his mouth.

"I can see how you made all this money you're supposed to have."

It was Lola's turn to laugh. "What do you know about all that?"

"I think the whole world knows about all that."

Lola shrugged. "Don't believe what you read in the papers. Most of it is hearsay. A lot of it bald-faced lies."

He chuckled at that. "Well, I'll give you the benefit of the doubt. But, all jokes aside, Lola," and his eyes lost all traces of humor, "this is something that I'm going to have to insist on. I have a young boy here that I'm doing my best to raise. And I've got a job to do and I don't want anything to interfere with that."

"Fair enough," she agreed, and she was pleased by the ripple of surprise that ran across his face. He had expected her to resist him. But she was much smarter than that. She wouldn't resist him now. But she would later.

She got out of her chair and turned so that he might have a good look at the soft curve of her rump. And when she was certain that she had his attention exactly where she desired it, she asked nicely, "I wonder where Jamie's gotten to?"

Chapter Six

"Jesus have mercy, boy! Get down from that window right this minute!" Annie said as the little boy clambered up to the open kitchen window and hung precariously from a piece of nicely whitewashed trelliswork.

In response, the child stuck his tongue out at her and said cheekily, "I don't have to do anything you say. You're not my mother."

"If I get my hands on you tonight—"

"My father said to make hot chocolate for me and lemonade for them," the boy interrupted.

Annie absorbed the information with a sniff. She hoped Lola knew what she was doing. The boy's father might turn out to be just as unpleasant and unruly as the child.

"Well, are you coming down from there? Or do I have to take a switch to your behind?"

"OK," the child said after a minute more spent hanging by just an arm and a leg. "I'll come down. But not because you told me to."

Annie muttered something heated beneath her breath and slapped a kettle onto the stove. She had been after Lola for years to get married and settle down. But she hadn't counted on having to deal with a demon seed offspring, too.

"Be careful how you get out from that—"

But her words were halted in her throat by a loud cry and the sight of a plummeting ten-year-old body.

"Oh lord," she said. "Jesus, lord, he'll break his neck."

Annie shoved her feet into a pair of worn leather slippers and pelted from the kitchen and down the short stone stairs.

"Boy, Jamie . . . where are you, child? Oh lord, he's probably killed himself. Broken his neck." Her eyes hunted the ground just beneath the kitchen window. "Jamie?" she called again, and then almost jumped out of her skin as a little head appeared in the kitchen window.

"Boo!" the child called cheerfully. "Gotcha."

It took several breaths to steady her heaving bosom, and then Annie pulled off a leather slipper and advanced. The child retreated, shrieking with laughter and calling an encouraging, "Betcha can't catch me. Betcha can't catch me."

This was the scene that Camille Roberts intercepted as she stepped from the elegant powder blue interior of her shiny BMW roadster. She barely managed to dodge the fleeing body of a little boy and then was almost run over by Annie Lewis as the housekeeper thundered after the child in hot pursuit, one slipper in hand and the other still on her left foot.

"Annie. Annie. Careful!" Camille called after the retreating woman. "My God, what is going on?"

Annie Lewis paused a short distance off and watched as the little boy disappeared into a thicket of trees. When she was sure that he wasn't coming back,

she turned and made her way back to where Camille
Roberts stood.

"What was that?" Camille asked, and she struggled
to maintain an appropriately serious expression.

"What was that? What was that?" Annie puffed.
"I'm going to wear out that little boy's backside, that's
what. Lola's getting herself in deep here. I don't know
if I want her to have this man after all."

Camille's eyebrows lifted. "You mean that's . . . the
boy? Chaz Kelly's boy?"

Annie nodded. "That's the little monster all right."

Camille nodded and gave a speculative, "Hmm. So,
where's Lola?"

Annie pressed a motherly hand against the small of
Camille's back.

"Come in and I'll tell you all about it."

"There he is now," Lola said, dropping the living room
blind back into place. "But he doesn't seem to have the
lemonade. I wonder what happened."

She walked to the front door with Chaz close behind.

"Jamie," Chaz said as soon as his son stepped through
the doorway. "What happened to you? I almost came
looking, you'd been gone so long. And what happened
to the lemonade you went off to get?"

The boy shrugged. "I got lost, and then it started
getting dark. So I came back so I wouldn't get mugged
or something."

Lola hid a smile. "It's OK, honey," she said. "There's
a big fence that runs around the entire property, so
there's not much of a chance that you'll be mugged here.

And don't worry about the lemonade. I'll go and—"

"No. Really. That's fine. We'll be perfectly OK without the lemonade, won't we, son?"

Jamie nodded.

"Are you sure? It really wouldn't be any trouble," and Lola wet her bottom lip in a suggestive little movement of her soft pink tongue.

"I'm sure."

"Can I invite you up to the house for dinner later on?"

"Thank you, but—"

"You've more unpacking to do," Lola finished for him.

"That and a few other things," Chaz agreed. Like calling his girlfriend, Audrey, for instance. It had been extremely difficult keeping her away from the entire moving-in process. But instinct told him that she, who was a sweet and wholesome soul, and Lola Barracuda St. James should probably never ever meet.

"I'll see you later, then," he said as Lola stepped out into the evening air.

"Yes, you will," Lola tossed over her shoulder. And, with that, she sashayed slowly back up the gravel path, her mind already churning over the problem at hand. She was going to get Chaz Kelly. There was absolutely no question about that. And when she did get him, maybe she'd make him pay just a little for putting her through all of this. He was going to moan like a babe once she finally got him between her very own satin sheets. . . .

Chapter Seven

"Oh God," Lola groaned. "Do you think the boy has mental problems? He seemed so sweet when I saw him earlier. I can't believe he was here. He told his father that he'd gotten lost."

"Well, he almost knocked me over when I arrived, so he was definitely here," Camille said, and she exchanged a little look with Annie.

"I'll tell you what that boy needs," Annie said, and she came to sit beside the two women seated at the center island in the kitchen. "It's that age-old remedy that never fails to work on children his age. The Bible speaks about it, too. You know, 'spare the rod and spoil the child'? What he needs is a serious dose of discipline. That's what he needs."

"Maybe he just likes you or something, Annie," Lola said. "Because I could hardly get a word out of him edgewise."

"Likes me?" Annie lifted herself from the stool. "You get him alone when his father's not around and see what you think then."

Camille laughed. "This could only happen to you, Lola." And she switched conversational streams with her characteristic fluidity. "So, have you noticed anything different about me yet?" she asked, and she wiggled the fingers of her left hand suggestively.

Lola grabbed her hand. "*No*. No, you didn't."

Camille beamed. "Yes, I did."

"Girl, are you crazy?"

Camille nodded. "Like a fox."

Lola examined the beautifully cut white diamond. "Why can't you work for your money like I did? Look at you. You have all of the right tools."

"That's what I was just telling her myself," Annie chimed in from her position before the stove.

Camille made a little sound of disgust. "I always told you that I was going to marry my money. So why're you so surprised?"

"But so quickly, Cam? I mean, do you think it's wise? And what about the age difference thing?"

Camille laughed heartily at that. "If people only knew how old-fashioned you really are, Lola St. James, you'd lose your rep in a minute."

Lola waved a dismissive hand. "Forget about my fashion for the moment. I know that man won't be able to satisfy you in bed. I mean there are pharmaceutical products out there now that can give him a little boost, but don't you want a young strapping man to wrap your legs about? And don't tell me that it doesn't matter, because I *know* you."

"I've thought about it. But I think I can struggle along with twenty point two million dollars."

Lola rolled her eyes. "Money again. I'm telling you, sweetheart, it's not going to work. There has to be—"

But Camille shushed her with a hand. "He's a nice

guy. I promise you'll like him. And don't be so hung up on age."

"Right," Lola said, and she folded her arms before her. "Didn't you tell me he had a walker?"

Camille chuckled. "A cane. Not a walker. And that's because he has a bad hip. Anyway," she said, and she gave her friend a good-natured little shove. "Enough about me already. How are we going to land this man you say you want? If things go right, we might be able to plan a double wedding."

"I don't know that I want to marry Chaz Kelly."

Annie turned from her pot of steaming black-eyed pea soup.

"Now don't start that nonsense all over again, Lola. You're not getting any younger. It's past time you made up your mind and settled. You're not a man, you know. *You* can't have babies when you're eighty."

"I don't think she wants to have babies at all, Annie," Camille chimed in smugly.

"Well, she's going after the wrong man then. 'Cause this one—"

"I know. I know," Lola snapped out. "He wants ten, fifteen children. God. Why is life so much harder for women?"

Camille tapped a nicely polished nail on the countertop.

"That's just the way things are, honey. So don't try to fight what you can't change. OK? Now, what's the plan?"

"Well, I'll tell you what I think," Lola said, leaning forward. She had her game face on now. And the expression in her eyes was one that many a tycoon had encountered across the expanse of her shiny board-room table.

"I'm going to need time alone with him, right? Lots of time alone with him."

"Right," the other women agreed.

"So," Lola continued. "Annie, this is where you'll come in. Now the child has obviously taken to you—"

Annie lifted a hand to the heavens and proclaimed: "No, lord. I'm not doing it, Lola. And don't even bother to try to persuade me, either, because nothing you can say will change my mind. It's made up. I won't do it."

"Annie . . ."

"I won't do it. I won't."

"Annie . . . think of my poor unborn babies. And you know I don't have that much time left, either."

"Using my own words against me is not right, Lola St. James. If you were that little boy's size I would turn you across my knee."

Lola gave the older woman a woebegone look, and Camille hid a chuckle behind a hand.

Annie dropped a bowlful of beef chunks into the pot of soup, spent a minute cutting up a handful of fragrant green shallots.

Lola smiled at Camille and lifted a finger to press against her lips.

"Well, what do you want me to do?" Annie turned to ask after she had stirred the pot in silence for a full two minutes. "And don't think I don't know what you're doing, either," she said, turning to wag a finger at Lola.

"You love me anyway." Lola beamed, and she beckoned Annie closer to declare, "OK. Here's the deal. . . ."

Across the lawns at the modestly sized guesthouse, Chaz was now bare-chested and vigorously involved in the process of disassembling large stacks of brown boxes. He pulled the sides out with the expertise of a man who had done this very thing many times before in his life, and then he crushed each box flat with the stomp of a foot. He did this steadily for several minutes before pausing to listen and then bellow, "Jamie, I don't hear any water running! Are you in that shower yet?"

Jamie sat on the edge of the thick cream-colored tub, still fully clothed, his head bent over a blinking and beeping handheld video game.

"OK, Dad!" he yelled back, reaching behind him to turn both taps to maximum volume.

Chaz nodded in satisfaction as he heard the shower start. Some parents had extremely bad kids, but he counted himself as one of the more fortunate ones. Jamie had rarely given him a single lick of trouble. And he was proud to say that he had never had to really spank the boy, either. He was just a very good little kid. He obviously didn't take after his father in that department.

A distant sadness crept slowly into his eyes. It had been years since he had thought about his ex-wife. Why should he suddenly think of her now? That Jamie never asked him any questions about her was something that he had always been extremely grateful for. How did a father tell his son that his own mother had not wanted to raise him? That his own mother had seen her child as a burden, an encumbrance to the joys of her high-flying, ritzy lifestyle. Even now, after all these many years, it made Chaz sad to think about it. Had he really been that bad of a husband to her? Had she ever really loved him? Had their entire relationship been about nothing more than money?

He sighed and went back to stomping the boxes. Women. He would never understand them. If it were completely up to him, he would probably never marry again. But he had to think about Jamie. It would be good for the boy to have the tenderness of a woman's care. Chaz had tried his best to be both father and mother to the child but was fully aware that there were still certain areas where he might be a bit lacking. A growing boy needed lots of affection. Lots of hugs and kisses. Things that a mother could do easily but a father . . . sometimes not so easily.

He bent to tie the first stack of flattened boxes, and his mind turned to Audrey. He didn't love her passionately. But he did like her. He liked her a lot. And maybe that would be enough.

He wiped his perspiring forehead against an arm, and a hoarse chuckle rumbled in his chest. Passion. What was he talking about? Was he a kid still wet behind the ears? Passion was for teenagers. Not grown men past the venerable age of thirty-five. He would never feel that kind of emotion again, and the sooner he realized it, the better it would be for him.

"Jamie!" he called, after he had finished on the last

pile of boxes. "I'm coming in to check, so make sure everything's clean."

The little boy who was still on the side of the tub gave a muffled response, dropped the video game on the tiled floor, and began the process of tearing the clothes from his body.

Chaz stacked the boxes neatly in the corner of the living room closest to the front door, wiped his perspiring brow on the white kitchen towel Lola had brought across with the sandwiches, and said, "Here I come, Jamie boy."

Chaz was halfway to the bathroom when the phone began to ring. Irritation rippled across his brow, and for a second he considered not answering it. He had told Audrey not to call him until after ten, so he knew that it couldn't be her. She always did exactly as he asked her to. So that left only one solitary person who would have the nerve to call at such a late hour. One solitary person who had probably never done as anyone had asked her to. Ever.

He snatched the phone from the hook and snapped a disgruntled, "Yes? Hello?"

Chapter Eight

At the sound of her voice, Chaz was taken aback by the brief wave of disappointment that swept through him. He rubbed a hand across his eyes and said, "Hello, dear. No, I'm not upset that you called." Lord, what was happening to him? He had actually wanted his caller to be Lola St. James.

He settled himself on the arm of a settee and spent the next several minutes going over the details of the move.

"Now see," Audrey said, and there were traces of pique in her voice, "I could've helped you do all of that. I still don't understand why you had to do the whole thing all by yourself. It's almost as though you don't even want me in your life."

Chaz gritted his teeth. Jesus Christ, not now. Not after such a long and hard day.

"Audrey . . . I've already explained all that to you. You said that you understood."

There was silence, and then the burgeoning sounds of sobbing.

Chaz chewed on the corner of his lower lip. What was this now? What had brought all this on? Audrey was always such a sensible young woman.

"Audrey? Sweetheart. Why're you crying?"

There was more sobbing, and then a voice he barely recognized as hers said in a muffled manner, "I just don't know where this relationship is going. You leave me out of some of the most important things in your life. You hardly spend any time at all with me. And then, when you do show up, you spend most of the time watching football on TV. What about me? Don't you care at all about me?"

"Yes, of course I care about you. You know I do," Chaz said, and then he placed the phone beneath his chin. "Jamie. Jamie!" he bellowed. "Get out of that bath right now. You've been in there for more than half an hour." He removed the phone from beneath his chin. "Sorry . . . Jamie's in the bath. You were saying that I don't spend enough time with you," he said, continuing smoothly. "So you're feeling neglected."

"That's it exactly," Audrey agreed in a sodden manner. "If you care about me like you say you do, then why can't you find more time for me in that busy life of yours? Everything and everyone is more important than me. Don't I count at all?"

Chaz softened his tone. "Of course you count, honey. You're my girl. You know that. And you know that everything I'm doing now is being done for you . . . for us."

"And that's another thing," Audrey said petulantly. "You keep hinting around about our future. About us getting married someday. Well, let me tell you. I'm getting to the point now where I'm just plain sick and tired of hints and innuendos and whatever other tricks you might have up your sleeve. We've been going out now for close to three years and I don't think we're any closer to the altar now than when we started out."

Chaz said a muffled, "Jesus," against the back of one hand and earned a wrathful, "What did you say?"

"I can't deal with this right now, Audrey."

"What?"

"I've got too much to handle." He scraped a hand across his close-cropped hair. "Can we postpone this discussion until tomorrow? I'll come by in the evening and we'll take a drive into D.C. Have dinner. Maybe see a show?"

Audrey sniffled. Well, at least that was something. She knew that she couldn't push him too far too fast. But she was tired of sitting around and just waiting for him to propose marriage. She would be thirty years old on her next birthday. And starting all over from scratch with another man entirely was not something that she looked forward to at all. Besides, men like Chaz Kelly didn't grow on trees.

"OK. But we have to have a serious talk about everything."

Chaz resisted the urge to sigh. "All right. We'll have a serious talk. I'll give you a call when I have a minute tomorrow. OK? Sleep well then." And he hung up the phone without bothering to wait for her response.

He walked toward the bedroom Jamie had selected with a swarm of thoughts rattling around in his head. He couldn't really blame Audrey for being upset. Women loved attention, especially from the significant man in their lives, and he hadn't been giving Audrey enough of that. Maybe he had started to take her for granted because she never complained about his treatment of her. But this was the woman he might marry someday soon, so why did he treat her as he did? She deserved better.

His forehead wrinkled. She deserved a man who really loved her.

He pushed open the bedroom door and a tired smile twisted the corners of his mouth. His son was propped up in bed reading a math book.

"Do I need to check behind your ears tonight?"

Jamie gave his father an innocent look. "Of course not, Dad."

Chaz came to sit on the bed. "Did you brush your teeth?"

Jamie folded the book on a finger. "Both up and down."

Chaz gave a pleased, "Hmm." Then, "Would you like a bedtime story tonight?"

Jamie chuckled. "Aw, come on, Dad. Bedtime stories are for babies. You know that."

Chaz reached forward to tickle his son about the ribs.

"Babies, huh?" he said in a threatening tone. And he proceeded to tickle his son until he had reduced the boy to a squirming and giggling tangle of limbs.

"Now what do you have to say about bedtime stories, young man?" Chaz finally asked.

"They're perfect for ten-year-olds?" the boy asked, his eyes sparkling with glee.

"That's right," Chaz said. "But I'll spare you tonight. But not tomorrow night," he warned.

Jamie nodded. "OK." Then, "Dad. Can we go to the movies tomorrow? Since it's Sunday?"

Chaz stood and shoved his hands into his pockets. "I may have to work late tomorrow, Jamie. You know I work on weekends, too." And at the child's crestfallen expression Chaz said, "But we'll see. All right?"

Jamie nodded. And as soon as his father had left the room and closed the door securely behind him, Jamie tossed the textbook in his hands onto the floor and then reached beneath the folds of the thick blanket for a comic book.

Chapter Nine

The first morning of summer roused Lola from a fitful sleep, and she turned onto her back and raised an arm to shield her eyes against the golden shards of sunlight. She gave the alarm clock a glance and then sat bolt upright. It was Sunday and Chaz Kelly was no more than a holler away. God, life was beautiful.

She rolled back her dainty pink comforter, stuck her feet into a pair of fuzzy bedroom slippers, and walked to the window to have a look at the day. She pushed the gauzy curtain aside, rolled up the venetian blinds, and allowed herself the luxury of a contented sigh. The sky was a clear blue. The sun promised a warm and balmy day. And already there was a soft wind blowing across the property.

Lola dropped the blinds back into place and then padded into the plush sitting room connected to her bedroom suite. She always greeted the day with music. Each day she selected a different CD. Luther. Barry. The Manhattans. But today, today she felt completely in sync with her destiny. Today she felt like . . . Ella. Sultry, sophisticated, elegant Ella.

She selected the CD, slid it into the stereo, and turned the music up to half its maximum volume. Then she went in search of clothes.

Halfway across the property, Chaz greeted the day with slightly less equanimity. He awoke with a thumping headache that only seemed to get worse as he inched his eyes open to the light. He had barely slept at all, and when he had managed to get some shut-eye his dreams had been filled with strange and confused images of Lola St. James.

"Damn woman," he muttered, and he rolled himself away from the bothersome rays of sunlight. The more he tried not to think about her, the more his contrary brain did just that. What was this strange power that she seemed to have over men? Was it natural?

He pulled the covers up over his head. God, he was losing his mind. Why was she having this kind of an effect on him? And after only one day, too. He squeezed his eyes shut and tried to force the throbbing away.

The other thing that bothered him was that unusual familiarity that pulled at him whenever she was around. He had noticed it for the first time when he was talking over the contract with her in her office. And then again yesterday when she had been in the house. There had been something. Something there. . . .

He coughed and then fought the urge to sneeze. Maybe he was just overtired. Overtired and in desperate need of a long, quiet vacation. He hadn't had one of those in years. Long days spent doing nothing at all but exactly what he wanted to do. Stretching out on a lawn chair or in a hammock, listening to the wind in the trees. These were simple luxuries that he had had none of for ages and that he would have none of for a very long time.

He sneezed heartily against his hand. God. That was

all he needed now. A cold. He cracked open an eye and took a look at his wristwatch. Almost seven-thirty. Another half an hour and he would get up, see about breakfast for Jamie, and then go take a look about the property. Lola St. James wanted a Jacuzzi pool put in, extensive landscaping done. More bushes and trees. A sanctuary with lots of flowers and shrubbery. He sneezed again and grimaced at the sandy feel of his throat. It would take a lot of work. But when he was through, it would be beautiful.

He closed his eyes again and sighed as his dreams took over. A soft hand against the sore patch of muscle in his back . . . ahhh, if only. . . .

"The senator called again," Annie said as she lifted a heavy round of dough from a large ceramic bowl and slapped it against the face of her kneading table.

Lola took a crunchy bite of muffin and then laid her newspaper down.

"Maybe I'll go out with him sometime next week."

Annie paused in her kneading. "What are you saying?"

Lola beamed. "It's all part of my plan. If there's one thing I've learned in business it's that you've always got to have leverage. Always."

Annie made a disbelieving sound beneath her breath. "I really don't understand all of these games that you young people play. In my day, if you were interested in a man, you let him know it. And if he wasn't so inclined, then you moved on and found somebody else. Somebody better. Maybe the senator."

Lola flipped to the business section of the newspaper and followed a line of stock with a finger.

"You know he's not right for me, Annie love," she said, after she had located the information she was after. "And besides," she said, lifting her head. "Can't you tell that Chaz needs me? And I don't mean financially, either."

"Well, maybe," Annie agreed, "but it's just that—" But her next words were interrupted by a loud call from just outside the window.

"Mrs. Lewis! Mrs. Lewis!"

Annie placed the dough in her hand on a baking tray and said, "Lord have mercy. The demon seed is back."

Lola bit back a chuckle and said, "Shh. Don't let him know I'm here. I want to see what he does."

Annie walked across to the window, pushed it open, and then leaned out to say, "Yes? What is it, boy?"

Jamie looked up at her. "Can you come out and play?"

Annie placed her floured hands on her hips. "Come out and play? Do you think I'm your age?"

Jamie pulled a slingshot from a back pocket. "Is the pretty lady at home?"

Annie shook her head. "No, she is not, though I don't know why that concerns you."

A spitball hurtled toward the windowpane and hit it with a smack.

Annie's startled gasp coincided with Lola's, "Oh my God." Another wet particle landed against the window and then another in rapid succession.

Lola ran to the large kitchen window and looked out. "Jamie!" she bellowed. "Stop that this minute."

The little boy seemed momentarily startled by her appearance, but he recovered nicely.

"Hello, ma'am. Mrs. Lewis and I are playing spit-ball tag."

"Don't you know how dangerous that slingshot is?" Lola spoke sternly.

"But Mrs. Lewis said that she wanted to play."

Lola folded her arms across her chest and attempted to appear as maternally severe as she possibly could.

"Mrs. Lewis said no such thing. And if I ever catch you doing anything like that again, I'm going to go straight to your father. Do you understand me?"

The boy's gaze battled with hers for an instant. "He won't believe you," he said finally.

Lola nodded. So he wanted to test her. This was something she knew how to handle.

"Do you want to give it a try?"

Jamie stuck the slingshot back into his pocket and gave her a belligerent stare. Lola folded her arms and waited.

"OK then, fine," the boy said after it became clear that she wasn't going to budge.

"And don't get into anything else, either," Lola warned as the child turned to go. "Or I *will* go to your dad."

"I don't care. He won't believe anything you say," the boy said, and with that, he turned and sprinted back up the gravel path.

Lola closed the kitchen window and turned to Annie.

"What is the matter with that kid? He's like a junior

delinquent in training. Doesn't Chaz discipline him at all?"

"I told you he's a little monster," Annie said, and she pounded the dough before her with particular ferocity. "What he needs is a good old-fashioned whipping. He has no respect at all for his elders."

Lola returned to her padded stool and propped her chin on a balled fist.

"God. This makes everything that much more complicated. What do I have to deal with now?" And she counted off on her fingers. "A man who won't give me the time of day. A very bad little kid, a—"

"Well, there's no point to that way of thinking, Lola honey," Annie interrupted. "Just like you always do, you've got to find a way through this."

Lola got up to press a kiss to the side of her housekeeper's face.

"So, you'll still help . . . even though . . ."

Annie gave a sniff. "Didn't I say I'd help you get this man? Do you think I change my mind that easily?" She sprinkled a handful of flour atop the round of dough. "So, this dinner now . . . how're we going to play it?"

Chapter Ten

Audrey Mackenzie rolled down her window and peered at the fancy gold lot number. A frown creased the smooth skin between her brows. She had decided to come all the way out from Washington, D.C., to see exactly where it was Chaz had moved to. She didn't really trust his long explanations about having to work and live on some woman's property. And the fact that he hadn't wanted her to help him move into his new place made her even more suspicious. She had wondered for a long time whether he had another woman. And she was tired of being the understanding girlfriend. If he was playing around with someone else, then she was going to figure a way to get him back. And figure a way to get him down the aisle. It was just that simple.

She turned her little Toyota into the mouth of the gateway and her eyes widened. Was this where he was living? In a mansion, with trees and lawns and water sculpture and tennis courts? Her lips pursed. Well, it didn't matter. She was going to meet this woman . . . Lola St. James and see exactly what it was that she was up against. She was certain that the woman couldn't match her in the looks department. In that area she knew that she was unsurpassed. Why, she could have been a model herself, if she had chosen to pursue that particular career path.

Audrey brought the car to a halt at the massive wrought-iron gates and rolled her window down even farther so that she might reach the button on the intercom.

"Yes, hello," she said as soon as her buzz was answered. "I'm here to see Chaz . . . Chaz Kelly. My name is Audrey B. Mackenzie."

"Just a minute," Annie said. She released the button and picked up the house phone. When Lola answered, she said, "Somebody called Audrey Mackenzie's at the gate."

Lola put down her writing pad, and a little smile touched the corners of her mouth. So, Chaz did have a woman after all. "Let her in."

Annie's brows wrinkled. "Let her in?"

"Yes, it's OK, Annie love. Let her in. I want to size up the competition."

Annie made a sound of disapproval beneath her breath and then went back to the intercom to say, "Can I ask what this is about?"

"I'm his . . . friend. Girlfriend," Audrey corrected. She wasn't about to demote herself. She was his girlfriend and would very soon be his wife.

Annie's lips tightened. "I'll let him know you're here."

"No. Don't," Audrey said quickly. "It's supposed to be a surprise. If you could just let me come in."

Annie's finger hesitated as the thoughts tumbled through her. What was Lola thinking, letting that woman in here before she had made any progress at all with Chaz? That was the problem with young people today. They didn't listen to the advice of older and wiser heads. Well, OK, Lola had said to let her in. So she would let her in.

Annie pressed the entry button and said, "Come on up. His house is down the drive and to the right. Once you get halfway, you can't miss it."

From her window in the library Lola watched the little Toyota hatchback come slowly up the gravel drive. And her eyebrows lifted as she caught sight of the woman behind the wheel. So this was her competition?

Lola went back to her desk, sat for a thoughtful minute, and then dialed Chaz's cell phone. As soon as he answered, she said briskly, "I'd like you to come up to the house, please. I've a few ideas about the project that I want to go over with you."

Chaz wiped a quantity of sweat from his brow with the back of his hand. "Well, I'm right in the middle of—"

"Right now, please," Lola said, and deliberately hung up the phone before he could voice another objection.

Chaz stared at the phone in his hand. She had hung up on him. The damn woman had hung up on him. He clipped the phone back onto his belt. Well, if she thought that he was going to jump through hoops for her, then she had a lot to learn about him. He was her employee, yes. But she had to understand that if they were going to work well together, she would have to learn to respect and—

He paused in mid-thought as a familiar Toyota came into view. Christ. What was she doing here? He didn't have the time for her right now.

He put down his clipboard of copious notes and walked slowly in the direction of the white car.

Audrey pulled the car into the little garage connected to the guesthouse and cut the engine. Well, she was here. And she would make the most of it. Chaz might be a little upset at first, but she would soon set that straight. She had brought lunch. Warm cornbread. Country fried chicken. Corn on the cob. Fruit punch. And peach cobbler for dessert.

She smiled and gave herself a final glance in the rearview mirror. Now, that was a meal to put any man in a good mood.

She climbed from the car, reached in for the cloth-covered wicker basket, and then straightened to take a look around.

The smile on her face blossomed as she caught sight of Chaz striding toward her. He was such a fine figure of a man. And when he was dressed in his blue jeans and T-shirt, there were few men on earth who could equal him in terms of raw sex appeal.

She waved a hand and called a very cheerful, "Surprise, honey!" If she hadn't been interested in getting him up the aisle, she would've topped off the little meal she had brought with her with a session of lovemaking. But she wouldn't. Men, even the good ones, had to be trained. And this was the best way she knew of to keep a man like Chaz Kelly under control. And the fastest way, too, to get him up the aisle and to the altar.

Chaz returned her wave and then glanced at his cell phone in irritation as it began to ring again. He was of half a mind to just ignore it, but after three rings he snatched it from his waist and barked a brisk, "Yes. Hello?"

Lola leaned back in her soft leather chair and swung her legs atop the desk.

"You're not here yet."

Chaz gritted his teeth. "I'm on my way right now." And this time *he* hung up. And pressing the disconnect button on his phone gave him a feeling of immense satisfaction. There was something about that woman that just got right under his skin. There was probably no other person on the planet who could make him feel such—

"Honey!" Audrey squealed, and she rested the basket at her feet and then sped across the short distance into his arms. She feathered his face with little butterfly kisses and then asked with a breathy note in her voice, "Are you happy I came?"

Before he could formulate an answer, his cell phone was ringing yet again. Chaz put Audrey away from him. This time, he wasn't going to answer it.

"Look, dear," he said. "Go into the house and make yourself comfortable. I have something to take care of."

Audrey pressed her lips together. "But, honey, I came all the way—"

"Just wait for me inside. I won't be long. All right?" he asked coaxingly.

"All right," Audrey said in a slightly petulant manner. "But why can't I come with you, wherever it is you're going?"

"Because I'm working. I have a meeting with the boss."

Audrey looked at him with suspicious eyes. "A meeting with your boss on a Sunday? Who works on a Sunday?"

"You know I work every day of the week." And he gave the tip of her nose a little tap, turned her, and sent her toward the house with a playful smack on the rump.

The phone rang again, and Chaz clicked it on.

"Yes. Lola."

Lola smiled at the tone in his voice. "I think you have a visitor. Why don't you bring her along with you?"

Chaz's brow wrinkled. "Bring her along? I thought you wanted to go over some things?"

The shrug was reflected in Lola's voice. "We can talk business for a few minutes, and then break for lunch."

"Ah . . . no," Chaz began, and then he sneezed heartily. "No. I don't think that's a good idea. If you don't mind, I'd prefer to just wrap things—"

"You have a cold?"

"What?"

Lola's heart pounded in her chest. This was her chance. This was her chance.

"You sneezed, so naturally, I wondered if you were coming down with an infection."

"I see," Chaz said. "And you're afraid of catching it, is that it? You want to postpone our little meeting?"

Lola laughed, and the sound of her husky voice caused Chaz to tighten his grip on the phone.

"I'll see you at the patio door. OK?"

And before Chaz could agree or disagree, she had hung up again.

"Rude woman," he muttered, and slid the phone back onto his belt.

Lola dialed the kitchen as soon as she disconnected the call.

"Soup, Annie. I need a big tureen of chicken soup. Some of your oven-fresh rolls. Warm salt water. And some of that cold medicine that makes you drowsy."

Chapter Eleven

Jamie crawled carefully along the branch and took a look in the open window. He watched as Audrey busied herself about the kitchen, warming the corn bread and chicken and pouring the red fruit punch into a large glass pitcher. He waited until she had washed her hands at the sink; then he dropped to the ground and crawled to the window. He watched her wipe her hands on a kitchen towel and waited patiently for her to leave the room. Then, when he was certain that she was no longer anywhere close by, he hoisted himself onto the whitewashed sill and crawled through the open window.

The child crept along the wraparound white counter to the cupboard where his father had stored the spices, pulled open the oak-finished door, and removed a short bottle of powdered jalapeño pepper. He shut the cupboard door again, listened for a minute, and then went on silent hands and knees to where the pitcher of fruit punch stood. His hands struggled for a moment with the tightly screwed cover; then the tea cloth that covered the mouth of the container was removed and half the bottle of pepper was emptied into the drink.

The boy chuckled as the powder sank slowly to the bottom of the jug. He gave the container a little shake, dipped his finger in to taste, emptied another portion of powder, and then sat bolt upright at the sound of his father's very stern, "Jamie, what are you doing?"

The child hid the bottle of pepper behind him and then gave his father an innocent, "Nothing."

Chaz came farther into the kitchen. "Don't give me that 'nothing' routine. What were you putting in that drink?"

The child's mouth set in an obstinate line. "I told you. Besides, it's a horrible drink anyway. Why does she have to bring us food all the time? She's not my mother."

Chaz's brows snapped together. "Get down from that counter right now, boy, before you make me come over there."

Jamie scrambled down and stood looking up at his father with bright, angry eyes.

"Now what is this all about? What's come over you all of a sudden?"

Jamie's hands balled into tight little fists. "Why can't . . ." His mouth worked. "Why can't my mother come and live here with us? Why don't you want her?"

Chaz stroked the curl of an ear with a finger. So that was what this was all about. Poor little kid. Chaz had been so wrapped up in trying to make enough money to take care of them both that he hadn't realized how much this entire situation of not having his mother around was affecting Jamie.

Chaz pulled out a straight-backed kitchen chair, sat, and then said, "Come here, Jamie. I should've said these things to you a long time ago, but I didn't think you were old enough to understand."

The child hesitated for a second, and Chaz assured

him in a voice completely devoid of all traces of anger, "It's OK, son. I'm not going to spank you."

A short while later, Lola was busy in the back of a large walk-in closet, rummaging about among dozens of garments. Annie bustled in pushing a nicely laid dinner cart before her. She set the brake on the cart and then called, "Lola?"

"Back here!" Lola yelled. Hangers continued to scrape for a few minutes more, and then she emerged holding a beautifully printed Oriental-style dress.

"What do you think of this?" she asked.

Annie rested her hands on her hips. "Is this for the dinner we're planning?"

Lola grinned. "It's for right now. I'm going to try something. A little test to see if he's really—"

But the pealing of the patio door chimes interrupted her, and she waved a hand at Annie.

"OK. He's here. Is everything on the cart? Great. Great." And she was through the bedroom door and down the short flight of stairs before Annie could say much in reply.

Annie stirred the soup in the thick cream-colored tureen and muttered to herself. If she lived to be a hundred years old, she would never fully understand the way Lola's brain worked. Talking about tests and asking for soup and salt water at a time like this. When what she should really be doing was figuring a way to get rid of the other woman who was even now nicely ensconced in Chaz Kelly's house. Why, it made no sense at all. No sense at—

"And this is Annie." Lola's voice caused the house-keeper to turn toward the open door.

Annie beamed, and she came forward to give Chaz a very warm hug.

"So you're the young man who's going to fix this place up?"

Chaz returned her smile with one of his own. "I'm going to try, Mrs. Lewis."

Lola gave a pleased nod. "He's the best at what he does. He told me himself."

Annie chuckled at the expression of embarrassment on Chaz's face.

"Lola's just teasing," she said. Then she motioned for Chaz to have a seat in one of the comfy settees.

"Sit down. Sit down. I know you have important business to talk over. So I'll just take myself off back to the kitchen." And she pressed one of Chaz's arms as she passed. "Now, don't be afraid to call me, if you need anything else."

Chaz sat, and his gaze drifted to the food cart and then back to Lola. He cleared his throat.

"You were saying you had some ideas?"

Lola walked to the cart and very calmly began to dish out a bowl of soup.

"I'll get to that in a second. But first, I'd like you to take this glass of salt water."

Chaz gave her a bewildered, "Glass of what?"

"Salt water. It'll be good for your throat."

"Look," Chaz began.

But she cut him off with, "Isn't your throat a bit sore?"

He met her eyes directly, and a reluctant smile curved the corners of his mouth. There was no question about it.

As unlikely as it was, his original suspicion about her appeared to be correct. Lola *Barracuda* St. James was definitely interested in him. He would have to let her down gently. Let her know that there was no chance on earth of there being anything other than a strictly professional relationship between them both. But how should he do it? Most women did not take kindly to any form of rejection. And with women like Lola St. James . . .

"Just try it," Lola coaxed. "It'll make your throat feel so much better. It's an old remedy I learned from my grandmother. It really works." And she proffered the glass.

Chaz took the glass. OK. He would humor her. It might make for an easier working relationship if he didn't appear to reject her completely. But sooner or later she would have to understand that he had absolutely no personal interest in her at all. He was going to marry Audrey. She was a fairly decent woman, a little demanding at times but decent. And that was what he needed in his life. A good woman.

"What do you want me to do with the salt water? Drink it? Because I have to tell you that may not go down too well."

"No. No. You gargle with it," Lola chuckled, and the raspy sound of her voice took Chaz completely by surprise. It was a warm, genuine sound, and he liked it.

He cleared his throat and stood. And for the first time he noticed that he was actually in a bedroom suite. *Her* bedroom suite. He pointed at a delicately painted peach-colored door that was partially open.

"Through there?"

Lola nodded. "Do you think you'll need any help?"

Chaz smiled at her, and Lola's heart thundered in reply.

"I think I can handle it."

Her smile was deliberately nonchalant. "All right. Remember to keep the liquid in the back of your throat for at least half a minute. And do that until the entire glass is done. OK?"

Lola finished ladling the soup and smiled to herself at the gargling sounds emanating from her bathroom. Now, if those weren't some of the most beautiful noises she had ever heard. Chaz Kelly, finally in her bedroom. Everything she had worked so hard for through the years had been leading to this.

She turned with expectation in her eyes as he reemerged from the bathroom with the empty glass in his hands.

"All done?" And she went to take the glass from his outstretched hand.

Chaz rubbed a hand along the length of his throat and said with some amount of bemusement, "Now isn't that something. It seems to have done the job."

Lola ushered him back toward a soft chair. "Now, for the soup," she said. And she waved a finger at him. "No objections now. It's been proven scientifically that chicken soup contains all sorts of antibiotics and other beneficial stuff."

Chaz accepted the bowl and sat back in his chair. He crossed his jeans-clad legs before him, took a spoonful of soup, savored it with enjoyment. Then in a pensive manner he said, "I know you're going to think this is crazy, but every time we talk face-to-face I get this odd feeling that we've met somewhere before. Have we?"

His question so startled Lola that she dropped the large silver ladle in her hand into the tureen of soup. She was forced to fish around in the broth for a full minute with a fork and spoon before managing to locate it.

Once she had, she placed the deep-bellied spoon on a side plate and pretended to busy herself with buttering one of the oven-warm rolls. Her hands scraped and spread the sweet yellow butter while her mind churned. So he hadn't forgotten her completely then? Even though she now looked different, there was still something about her that had jogged his memory. This was surprising. Surprising and good.

When she was through with the roll, she took a bite of it and then forced herself to say very calmly, "What an interesting thing to say. Maybe I remind you of someone from your past. Do you think that could be it?"

Chaz sampled another spoonful of soup and Lola waited on tenterhooks for his reply.

"I don't think I've ever known anyone quite like you." He scratched the side of his face. "That's why the whole thing is so strange. I've never had this happen to me before." He laughed again and then looked at her with bland eyes. "It's probably just my imagination. Or my severely overtired brain."

Lola pounced on that, anxious to be off the topic of who she reminded him of.

"Maybe what you need is someone to help you relax."

Chaz drank some more soup, thought about how to reply to such an obviously flirtatious comment, and then decided to just bite the bullet.

"Lola," he said, and there was a certain gentleness

in his voice. "I should tell you that I'm involved with someone right now. . . ."

Lola rested her half-eaten roll on the cart. She had anticipated the arrival of this very moment, but now that it was here, she could barely manage to contain herself.

"I also know that you're having some trouble getting your business going. And that you probably won't be able to get married to your . . ." She was loath to say the words. ". . . your friend before you manage to stabilize your affairs."

Chaz said nothing. He could sense exactly where the conversation was going and was well aware that there was treacherous territory just ahead.

Lola walked into the closet and lifted the Oriental print sundress from its hanger. She pulled the T-shirt over her head and then stepped out of her jeans.

"What I really wanted to talk to you about is . . ." And the rest of what she said was muffled by the slide of fabric across high cheekbones, a perfect nose, and softly pouted lips.

Chaz massaged his temples with the middle finger and thumb of one hand and tried his best to think above the dull thud that had started somewhere near the base of his skull. God almighty, what had he gone and gotten himself involved in now?

"I'm sorry . . . what?" he asked, and he tried his best not to look in the direction of the walk-in closet. Whatever it was she was doing in there was absolutely no concern of his.

Lola emerged in the short dress and Chaz sat bolt upright as she turned and presented him with the yawning back of the dress and a considerable length of ultra-smooth dark berry flesh.

She cast a glance at him over the round of a shoulder and said in a manner that Chaz was certain Eve must have used on Adam on that infamous day, "Can you help me with the zipper?"

Chapter Twelve

Chaz hesitated for half a second, and then he grabbed ahold of the black-headed zipper and yanked it toward the neckline of the dress, taking great care not to touch any of the exposed flesh as he did so. Then he stood and said in a slightly winded manner, "I think it might be best if I came back tomorrow . . . when you're in more of a businesslike mood."

Lola turned with sparkling eyes. This was going much better than even she had hoped. She met his gaze with a bold look.

"Am I making you nervous?"

Chaz laughed, but the sound cracked in his throat. "That's not exactly how I would describe it." And he plowed on as she prepared to speak again. "Look, Lola. I'm going to have to be honest with you. This . . . this thing is not going to happen between us."

Lola smiled at him. "Before you make any rash decisions, why don't you at least listen to my . . . ah, proposal?" She motioned for him to be seated and when he had settled himself again, continued. "I promise you that what I'm about to say will be of a strictly business nature."

Chaz cracked his knuckles. "OK. I'm listening."

Lola walked slowly back to the food cart, picked up her bowl of soup, and sampled a spoonful.

"I have an offer to make."

"Go on."

"You know of course that I am a modern self-made woman."

Chaz nodded. He still didn't trust the conversational direction. And, at the present moment, he trusted his body even less. In his younger years, with much less provocation, he would have taken that flimsy slip of a dress right off of her. He wiped a bead of perspiration from his temple.

"And," Lola continued, "I have . . . shall we say . . . certain needs."

Chaz coughed loudly, and Lola went to the food cart and poured him half a Dixie cup of medicine.

"Drink," she said. "You'll feel all right in about half an hour."

Chaz took the cup and drank with the distinct feeling that he would somehow never again feel *all right*.

"You were saying?" he grated, and he wiped the leavings of the amber medicine on the back of his hand.

Lola took the cup from him and continued as though her conversation had not been broken for at least a few minutes.

"And what I'm looking for is a modern yet simple way to satisfy these needs . . . in a discreet and adult fashion."

Chaz rubbed the curl of an index finger against the blunt of his nose. Well, if that didn't just beat everything. This woman was unlike any he had ever met before. And he had met some women in his time. Especially during his wild early days in the NFL when the promise of life had been sweet.

"Lola," and he tried to think of the best way to put it, "I think I probably used to be the kind of guy that you're obviously looking for." He flexed his fingers. "But that wild young man is gone. All I want out of this job that you so . . . ah, thoughtfully offered me is the money I'm entitled to, and your recommendation on a job well done. I'm really not trying to get involved in anything else. So, as tempting as your offer is . . ." He laughed in a rueful manner. "And believe me, it is tempting. I'm afraid—"

"You haven't heard my entire offer yet. Just hear me out," she said as he prepared to rise to his feet yet again.

"I think you may have gotten the wrong impression. I know that you're not the kind of guy who could ever become any woman's gigolo." She wrinkled her nose. "I hate that word. It's so crude. What I'm suggesting is nothing anywhere near that indelicate. I'm proposing nothing more than a mutually beneficial arrangement, whereby you keep your self-respect and I, similarly, keep mine. And, at the end of the period, we both walk away free and clear . . . no strings, no hurt emotions. Since it won't be about love and marriage. Just a quid pro quo kind of arrangement."

This time Chaz came to his feet, and there was an indecipherable expression in his eyes.

"I know that you're not used to being turned down, so I'm going to say this as gently as I know how, and then we will both agree never to mention it again. I'm involved in a serious relationship with a woman I—"

"With a woman you don't love." Lola nodded. "A woman who doesn't inspire you to passion. A woman who has a similar lukewarm feeling for you?" Her eyes flashed at him in sudden anger. "Don't you want to feel passion again? Have you lost all of the fire you used to have?"

His brows snapped together and for a moment Lola thought that she had gone too far. She had already said a lot more than she should have. Calling him passionless, weak, suggesting that maybe she did know him a lot better than she had let on. Her heart thundered as a crowd of sudden thoughts hit her. Had she pushed him too far, too fast? Would he pack his things and leave? Would he break the contract under grounds of harassment, toss the million dollars she had enticed him with right in her face, and leave? Well . . . well, if he tried that, she would . . . she would just have to stop him. She would use every resource she had access to if she had to.

His eyes met hers across the short distance, and Lola's heart trembled. In those midnight black eyes she saw strength, integrity . . . anger. God. What had she been thinking? Was she losing her touch? This was not the way to get to him. This was not the way to get him to give up his other woman.

Chaz removed his hands from his pockets.

"You're accustomed to being in control, aren't you, Lola St. James? Accustomed to having things your way all the time. Isn't that right?"

Lola cleared her throat. Swallowed to get rid of the sudden dryness. She didn't like the tone of his voice one little bit.

"I presented you with a clear-cut proposition."

He shifted his stance and said in a conversational manner, "Well, it's not that clear-cut to me. Let's just rewind for a bit. You want us to have an affair."

"That's right," Lola said, and her eyes sparkled with challenge.

"A mutually beneficial arrangement, you said?"

"Yes."

"And you get what out of it?"

"Sex . . . among other things," she said in a muffled manner.

"And I get . . . what . . . ? Beyond the obvious, of course?"

Lola dipped her spoon into the now-cool soup, lifted it to her lips. She didn't trust where this was going. She suspected that he was setting her up, but for what exactly, she didn't really know.

"You get a chance to be introduced to some of the movers and shakers in the industry . . . because I'll make sure that you meet them. You'll get some other projects. . . ." Her words flowed quickly as the ideas hit her. "Loans that you couldn't get before you'll find you have no problem . . . ah, obtaining. And once we decide to go our separate ways, you'll be able to marry your . . . your friend."

Chaz stroked a finger against the curve of his jaw. "And why should you want to do this for me?"

She almost choked on another spoonful of tepid soup but managed a very calm, "Believe me, it's more for me than it is for you. I'm sure you've heard the rumors about Senator Mason and me?" She surged on as he drew breath to speak.

"I'm interested in marrying Senator Mason, of course, but he has very old-fashioned ideas about love and marriage." She put the bowl down and gave him a very direct look. "He comes from an old Southern family, and . . . ah, you know how people from down South are?"

She looked at him and could tell by the lack of expression on his face that he hadn't a clue what she meant.

"What I mean is, he doesn't believe in, ah . . . premarital relations. And I'm a grown woman with—"

"With needs. I know," he interrupted.

Lola's eyes darted to his face. Was he laughing at her?

"Yes. Anyway. So there you have it," she said after a moment. "If you give me what I need, I'll give you what you want." And she sat back in her chair to give him her most businesslike look. "It seems like the perfect exchange to me. And of course, everything will be completely discreet. No one else will know about this . . . this arrangement . . . except Annie, and we can trust her."

Chaz laughed then, and Lola was relieved to see that the anger had all but filtered away from him.

"I must be living in a totally different world," he said. And he rubbed a hand across his eyes and appeared so tired and run-down that it was all Lola could do to remain where she was.

"So what do you think?" Her voice was brisk although what she wanted more than anything was to walk across to where he stood and offer to massage away the headache she could see he was hiding.

"I've never had a more interesting offer. But you, Lola St. James," and he looked at her as though he was really seeing her for the very first time, "you don't need to do this. You're a beautiful woman. Any man would be more than happy to have you . . . if only for a brief time."

He gave a hacking cough, swallowed with some difficulty, and then continued, "What you should do is talk it over with your . . . Senator Mason, and see if you can work things out."

Lola wet her lips in a little unconscious motion. "What are you telling me?"

"I guess what I'm saying is . . . you don't need me. Not for something like this."

Lola stood. "But *you* need me. You do," she said as he got ready to object. She closed the short distance that separated them both, lifted a soft hand to rest against his cheek. "Don't you understand that what I'm offering you is what all men dream of? No-strings sex. How can you beat that? Besides, you're sick . . . and you look so tired. Let me take care of you. I know exactly what you need."

Chaz lifted a calloused hand to cover hers and for one brief, giddy moment Lola thought that she had done it. She had won. But instead of caressing the warm, soft flesh that was pressed against his cheek, he removed it. And in a grating manner said, "The timing here is all wrong."

He turned her hand over and touched the center of her palm with a hard and calloused thumb. "If we were to be together, though, it would be because I wanted to be with *you*. And not because of some clinical business arrangement. And definitely not because I wanted something or the other from you. Do you understand?"

And at her brief nod, he stroked her palm again. Lola sucked in a tight breath and tried her best to control the curl of heat the simple touch caused in her lower abdomen.

"Now I've got to get going, OK?" And he looked at her in a gentle manner. "I've kept my . . . guest waiting long enough."

Lola watched him go with simmering eyes. So he had passed the test. But damn. Damn. Damn. She had never been turned down by a man before. What was this all about? Was she beginning to lose her touch?

She picked up her half-eaten roll and took a hefty bite. Well, she wasn't halfway to being beaten yet. By the time she was through with him, Chaz Kelly would be completely and totally whipped. And now that she knew he was a man of integrity, all of her doubts were gone. She *was* going to keep him. So Audrey B. Mackenzie was going to have to go . . .

Chapter Thirteen

"Where exactly have you been?"

Chaz closed the door behind him and tossed the front door keys onto a table next to the door.

"I told you where I was going."

Audrey's eyes glittered with latent anger. She was just sick and tired of being treated this way. And this time, this time he wasn't going to get away with it. Here it was, she had cooked him a nice meal, had driven for more than a whole hour in heavy traffic just to see him, and what did he do as soon as she arrived? Run off to spend hours on end with some other woman.

Audrey's eyes flickered over him. And if that weren't bad enough, by the looks of things he had had more than just a *talk* with his so-called boss, too.

Her nails curved painfully into the flesh of her palm. If she hadn't been properly raised, she would have slapped that innocent look right off of his face. His entire routine about trying to live the right kind of life for his boy just made her sick.

"Do you know how long you were gone? I brought you lunch. Now it's almost time for dinner. But do you care about that? Do you care about me? I'm just so tired of the way you treat me." And she grabbed at his arm as he began to walk around her. "Don't you dare walk away from me when I'm talking to you. We're not finished yet."

Chaz looked at her with cold eyes. "We just might be if you keep this up. Where is my son?"

Audrey propped her hands on her hips. "Where is your son? Where is your son? Have you been listening to a single thing I've been saying?"

"I'm not up to this right now, Audrey. I think I'm coming down with a—"

"Of course you're not up to it," she snapped as he turned away from her again. "Sex has a way of wearing you out. Wearing you down. So it's no wonder you look run-down like that all the time. That's right. I said it," she spat. "And don't think for a second that I don't know what you're probably doing up here every night while I'm all the way out there in D.C."

"Audrey. Be careful that you don't say something you regret later."

His tone held a latent warning, but Audrey was too upset to pay any attention. She paced the floor before him like an angry tigress.

"I've been keeping a lot of things inside me all of these years. A lot of things that you really need to hear."

Chaz reached out to take her by the shoulders. "You're upset," he said. "And maybe you're entitled to this. I haven't been there for you the way I should have been. But I promise you, all of that is going to change. Life for us is going to be so much better. If things go the way I think they will, by next year this time, we'll be—"

Audrey lifted a hand. "I don't want to hear it. I'm really, really tired of all of your promises." She sucked in a tight breath and struggled to control the tumble of words. If she really let loose and let him know what she thought of him and his spoilt rotten kid, he might never speak to her again. And that would dismantle all of her plans for him.

"Let's just," and she made a valiant attempt to control herself. "Let's just get ready to go, OK? Maybe what we need is a night out. I brought a change of clothes with me. Did you make arrangements for a sitter?"

Chaz gritted his teeth. He had a thumping headache, the soreness at the back of his throat was coming back, he was drowsy from the medicine he had taken at Lola's place, and he had forgotten all about promising to take Audrey out.

"Look, Lola . . . ," he began. "I'm really not feeling up to going anywhere. . . ." And he paused at the expression of stunned shock on Audrey's face.

Her hands balled on her hips. "What did you call me? What exactly did you call me? Lola?" And she spun on her heel and headed for the kitchen. She'd been right. God, she'd been so right. He was messing around with this . . . this Lola woman. Well, she wasn't having any of it. She had played the sweet little miss for more than long enough.

At the kitchen sink, she turned the cold-water tap on full blast and stuck both of her hands beneath the running water. She needed time to think. If she made the wrong move here, everything would crumble. And if she made no move at all, he would continue treating her as though she didn't matter *and* he would continue sleeping with this Lola person.

Audrey splashed a handful of cold water into her face. It was just so damned frustrating having to play the part of the understanding girlfriend. She didn't care about what he was going through. She had enough of her own problems to deal with. And if he thought for even one solitary minute that she was going to put up with him having another woman, he had a lot to learn. *A lot to learn.*

She turned the water off as another thought struck her. Why hadn't he followed her out to the kitchen to console her? Hadn't he just called her by some other woman's name? How dared he treat her like that?

Her eyes fell on the jug of fruit punch and the covered platter of country fried chicken and corn bread. OK. Fine. So he wanted to play like that. Fine. She would take her food and go. Let him cook his own dinner.

She snatched up the pitcher of red juice and poured it back into the flask she had brought with her. If he wasn't going to take her out for dinner as he had said he would only last night, then she would have this food that she had slaved over.

She placed the platter in the wicker basket and secured the golden latch on its side. Then she opened her Coach bag, rolled a fresh coat of lipstick onto her already-red mouth. With basket in one hand and flask in the other, she went in search of him.

"Chaz? Chaz?"

There was a moment's pause and then, "I'm in the bedroom."

She followed the sound of his voice and came to stand in the arch of the bedroom doorway.

Chaz was lying beside his son, and the boy was fast asleep and making endearing little grunts from a half-open mouth.

At the sound of her, Chaz removed an arm from across his eyes and said, "I'm sorry. I'm not feeling so hot and I don't have the energy right now to continue our talk." His eyes flickered to the basket in her hands. "Are you leaving?"

Audrey tilted her chin up. So he was going to be his usually calm self and pretend that they weren't having a fight.

"Yes. I'm leaving," she said in a stiff little voice.

He sat up carefully and swung his legs onto the carpeting so as not to wake the sleeping child. Audrey tightened her lips. He probably wasn't sick at all.

"I'll walk you out," he said.

She tightened her grip on the basket and her anger intensified that much more. He hadn't even tried to kiss her since she had arrived. Not even a little peck on the cheek. What kind of a relationship were they having? Were they brother and sister? And yet he had the nerve to say that he really wanted to marry her? Was this the way he envisioned their marriage? With him totally ignoring her, working a hundred hours a day every day of the week, while she, the good little wife, would be stuck at home tending to his spoilt rotten kid? Well, once they got married, he would soon understand that she had no intention of living that way. She would put up with him during this ridiculous courtship of his, but once she was his wife, a lot of things were going to change. The first one being sending the boy off to military school.

Her lips trembled with anger.

"Don't bother seeing me to the door."

And she turned and walked briskly back down the

shiny parquet floor, listening hard to see if he was behind her. At the front door she turned to look; then she wrenched open the whitewashed door and slammed it behind her. Hard.

Chapter Fourteen

Lola was up bright and early on Monday morning. It had been ages since she had worked from her office in Rockville, but this morning she had a slew of important things to attend to and she preferred to handle them all in the place where she had closed some of her biggest deals. She also wanted to review the extensive file of information she now had on a few of the banks in the Washington, D.C., area.

She bustled quickly about the suite, opening drawers, turning on music, and then finally heading into the large walk-in closet.

She chose a pin-striped navy blue suit with single-breasted buttons and a short skirt. Her blouse was crisp and white, her stockings, sheer. She spent ample time sitting on a padded stool before her dressing table creaming her face and then skillfully applying the barest hint of black eyeliner, a touch of color, and gloss. She pinned her hair into a tight roll, allowing a few soft strands of hair to escape at her temples, and completed the entire look with a gentle spritz of fragrance behind each ear.

At almost exactly a quarter of eight, she was walking briskly down the central staircase that opened into the front foyer, with patent-leather briefcase in hand.

The aroma of smooth Blue Mountain coffee drifted from the kitchen and she clipped in that direction. Annie looked up as soon as she entered.

"I have coffee, muffins, and Spanish omelets this morning. And don't tell me that you're not hungry, either. It's just not good, the way you young people eat. . . ." And Annie drew breath to say some more.

Lola rested her briefcase on the floor and then went across to kiss Annie soundly on the cheek.

"Don't fret, Annie love," she said. "You know I eat the way I do so I can keep this great figure." She gave her firm abdomen a little tap. "Besides, how else am I going to get that troublesome man up the lane?"

"Well, it doesn't seem to be doing you that much good so far," Annie sniffed.

Lola went to perch herself on the edge of a padded stool. She beamed at her housekeeper. "Not yet," she said. "But that's only because I had to find out the kind of man that he is. You know?"

Annie brought over a mug of cream-laced coffee and Lola accepted it with thanks.

"Now that I know what he's really like . . . what he'll go for, I can properly plan stage two. And believe me when I tell you, no man on earth can withstand my kind of stage two."

Annie went to the fridge, selected a pitcher of Lola's favorite juice, poured a glass.

"You and your stages," she said, shutting the fridge door. "Sometimes I don't know if I'm coming or if I'm going with you. So what are you having?"

And the expression on her face made Lola quickly say, "I'll have some of your beautiful Spanish omelet, and a slice . . . two slices of wheat toast." She amended this as Annie prepared to launch into the virtues of having bread in the morning.

Lola tucked into the meal as Annie went over the daily *to-do* list with her.

"Uhm," Lola agreed as she swallowed another savory forkful of omelet. "I really think we should redecorate that room on the far side of the house. I've been thinking about turning it into a playroom. That way I'll be able to have the little . . . monster under your watchful eye while his father works. In fact," and her eyes gleamed with sudden enthusiasm, "I'll make the call to the interior decorators when I get into the office. What d'you think?"

Annie poured herself some apple juice, placed a warm omelet on a breakfast plate, and then came over to sit.

"I know you have to focus a lot of your attention on the father . . . for obvious reasons, but I really think that what that little boy needs is a mother's love. Your love."

Lola gave her a startled look. "You almost sound as though you like the little truant."

"Well," and Annie took a refreshing swallow of juice, "he's just a little boy, after all. Didn't you tell me that the poor thing's mother abandoned him young? Just up and left him?"

Lola nodded. "I don't even think she looked after him for a single day. I think the story is that after she left the hospital, she just handed the kid over to Chaz . . . and that was it."

Annie crunched on a slice of toast. "That's exactly

what I'm saying then. Maybe that's why he behaves that way. And since you are going to be his new mother," she gave Lola a stern little look, "you have to begin building a relationship with the child now. You can't wait until after you all are married. Because if you do . . . lord help you."

Lola nodded. It made sense. It all made sense. But, good God almighty, the little boy was such a handful, and she already had enough to handle with Chaz.

"I'll try after I get to stage three with Chaz, but now I need your help, Annie. You really understand children. You know how to handle them . . . even the bad ones like our Jamie boy."

Annie scraped back her stool. She hadn't the same level of confidence in her ability to control this particular child. But only time would tell.

"You had enough?"

"That's it for me," Lola said, and she patted the corners of her mouth with a linen napkin. She took a moment to roll on a fresh coat of color and then bent to retrieve her case.

"I'll be back before five . . . unless the traffic's really bad."

"Dinner at seven?"

Lola nodded. "Dinner at seven."

A fond smile drifted into the housekeeper's eyes as Lola breezed through the front door and walked crisply toward her black Jeep Cherokee. This was the Lola who had conquered the business world. This was the woman who could make just about anything happen.

Annie shook her head and went across to the sink. Chaz didn't have a chance. . . .

Chapter Fifteen

An hour later, Lola sat at her desk with the phone pressed to her ear. She had caused quite a stir when she arrived at her office. Her personal assistant, Ronnie Childs, greeted her at the door with an expression of concern on her face. She was well aware that Lola never came into the office unless there was a problem. A big problem. But after a few minutes of Lola explaining what it was she needed, Ronnie was convinced that nothing catastrophic had happened and things settled back into their natural rhythm.

With the assistance of two of Lola's most trusted employees, the required box of files was located and carted into her office. And, over a second cup of coffee, Lola settled herself behind her desk and began flipping through the pages of neatly arranged information.

She began making calls as soon as she had put together a long list of names and phone numbers. Halfway into her first call to the CEO of one of the largest banks in the area, she suddenly interrupted her flow of conversation to ask nicely, "Jack, can I put you on hold for a minute?" And having secured his approval, she pressed the hold button on the phone and then called to her assistant in the outer office.

"Ronnie, can you find the phone number and address of Audrey B. Mackenzie, please? I believe she lives somewhere close to Howard University."

Her assistant appeared in the doorway. "A potential client?"

Lola laughed at the suggestion. "No," she said. "This is a personal matter."

Ronnie Childs, who had been through many a hostile maneuver with Lola, gave her boss a conspiratorial wink and an, "I got you."

Lola spent half the morning on the phone, going almost machinelike from one call to the next. Until she finally reached the very bottom of her call list. It was the last bank she had selected, and the most important, because this was where Chaz had most recently applied for a small business loan.

She turned her chair toward the large glass window and stared out at the beautiful summer day. Based on her calls around town, she had discovered that Chaz had attempted to secure loans from most of the banks in the area. And the final bank on her list had received his loan application just a few days before.

She twirled her pen between her long fingers and then turned in her chair to pick up the phone. She dialed quickly and then sat back in the plush leather chair. The phone was answered after only two rings, when an efficient-sounding female voice said, "Good afternoon. Mr. Abraham's office."

Lola smiled. "Hello, Ruth. It's Lola. Let me speak to Andy, please."

The woman's voice warmed. "Miss St. James. What a nice surprise. We haven't spoken in a while."

"Well, I took a short vacation in May. . . ." And for

the next several minutes Lola exchanged pleasant chitchat with the bank president's executive secretary. She inquired about the woman's husband, whom she had met at a bank function earlier in the year, and spent a bit of time congratulating her on how well her twins, who were both in high school and engaged in an accelerated program of study, were doing.

And when finally the executive secretary sensed that it was time for the small talk to end, she said, "It's been so very nice talking to you. Let me transfer you to Mr. Abraham now. I know that he's anxious to say hello."

Lola thanked the woman, assured her that she would indeed be speaking to her again soon, and then waited with some amount of impatience for her call to go through.

"Andy," she said as soon as her call was picked up. "Listen. I have a small favor to ask. . . ."

On the other side of town, Chaz was involved in a few delicate negotiations of his own. He had gotten out of bed at six-thirty, cooked a breakfast of singed pancakes and bacon, showered, dressed, and then gone in to wake his son.

"But, Dad," Jamie had complained in a very drowsy voice, "why do I have to shower again today? Jamal said that—"

Chaz hid a reminiscent grin. He had never been that keen on showering, either. But with what he hoped was appropriate parental steel, he rolled back the blanket and sheet and said solidly, "Come on, young man. How do you expect to get yourself a girl one of these days if you don't get accustomed to keeping yourself clean?"

Jamie sat up, rubbing the sleep from his eyes, and said in a sulky manner, "I don't even like girls. They're all mean and nasty."

"You say that now, but you won't think so in a few years," Chaz said. And he gave Jamie a playful slap with the towel that hung about his neck. "Come on," he said. "I won't have anyone saying that I don't take good care of my boy."

An hour later, the child was bathed, dressed, and standing in Chaz's tiny bathroom as the areas behind his ears were inspected.

"Are you sure you took a shower?" Chaz asked again, and he wiped at the skin around Jamie's neck with a white washcloth.

"Yes, Dad," Jamie said, and he gave his father his most innocent look.

Chaz wiped again and then flung the washcloth into the sink.

"Take that shirt off. It's dirty. And go and wash your face and neck again. No. Do it right here where I can see you," he said as the child made a beeline for his own room.

After fifteen minutes and a thorough session of scrubbing with cloth, soap, and water, Chaz inspected the ears and neck again and nodded in satisfaction.

"Now that's more like it. And from now on, if you don't do a good job washing yourself, I will watch you while you shower. Understand me?"

The child nodded and then changed direction with mercurial speed.

"Dad, can I just stay here today? I don't feel like going to summer camp."

Chaz squeezed a length of toothpaste onto his brush, turned on the cold-water tap.

"You want to stay here? With me?"

Jamie played with a curl of carpeting. "I won't be any trouble."

Chaz bent his head to scrub. "The equipment and other supplies are arriving today," he said between sweeps of the brush across his teeth. "I won't have the time to keep an eye on you."

"Maybe Mrs. Lewis can?" The boy's voice was hopeful.

Chaz rinsed with a glass of water, wiped his mouth on the towel about his neck.

"Mrs. Lewis has enough work to do. I'm sure she doesn't have the time to keep an eye on you, either."

"What about the pretty lady, then?"

Chaz laughed. Lola? Keep an eye on his kid? That was the last thing that she would probably ever agree to do. The woman only really cared about two things. The first was making money, and the second, making even more money.

"No, Jamie. If you really don't want to go to camp, then maybe . . . just this once we can see if Mrs. Lewis can watch you. But mind you don't give her any trouble," and he held up a finger to emphasize the point. "None at all. You get me?"

Jamie beamed. "Can I take my cards and other stuff over to the big house?"

· · ·

At close to noon, Ronnie Childs popped her head into Lola's office and said in a very pleased manner, "I've got that address and phone number. Should I call her to set up an appointment?"

Lola motioned her forward as the phone on her desk began to ring again. She stretched her hand for the slip of paper in her assistant's hand and then picked up the phone.

"Lola St. James." She paused and then said, "Annie. What's happened?"

She listened some more, nodding her head from time to time.

"He asked you to watch him? All day? Well, that's perfect. That means you won't have to offer." And Lola chuckled heartily at Annie's response. "It won't be so bad," she consoled. "If he really gets out of hand, then we'll have to tell Chaz, but I don't want to do that just yet." She nodded and assured, "I know what I'm doing. I promise you. It's all going to happen. I'm working on the next stage right now." She glanced at the slip of paper in her hand and answered Annie's query with: "No. No. Not on the phone. I'm going to go see her. Yes. In person." She hung up the phone with a final, "Don't worry," and then called to her assistant again.

"Ronnie," she said as the woman appeared in the doorway. "I have to make a quick trip into D.C. I may be back or not. Either way, if Andrew Abraham from East Coast Bank calls, transfer him to my cell. And of course if Annie calls again, tell her I'll be fine. She'll know what I mean. Also, call that . . . Audrey Mackenzie person and make sure she's at home. Then let me know."

Ronnie Childs nodded and scribbled on her pad. Whatever was going on was something so big that not even she was being let in on any of the details. But she knew when to question her boss and when to keep her mouth shut.

Lola gathered a few papers, inserted them into her briefcase, cast a final look about her desk, and said, "Put these back under lock and key, will you, Ronnie. I don't think I'll be needing anything else."

Within a few minutes, she was back in her Jeep and merging with the lunch-hour traffic.

Chapter Sixteen

The neighborhood was an interesting blend of wooden three-story buildings with short whitewashed walk-ups pressed closely together with large brick-faced brownstones with neat little flower boxes lining the stoops and window ledges. Cars of all sizes and descriptions lined either side of the street, and Lola craned her neck, looking at one side of the street and then the next, searching for an open spot. Her brow wrinkled. This was what she hated most about life in the city. There was never anywhere to park. There were always way too many people and not enough space.

She slowed the Jeep, cranked the window down, and then called out to a group of young men leaning on the side of a large seventies-model car, "Do you know where Twenty-one and a half is?"

A tall, rangy youth with baggy clothes and cornrows detached himself from the others and came over.

"Who you looking for?" he asked. And then, as he caught sight of Lola, he took a dramatic step backward to declare, "Damn. You're fine."

Lola grinned at him. She had grown up in neighborhoods much like these, and she understood the code.

"You're not so bad yourself."

The young man leaned on the car. "This your ride?"

"Do you know Audrey Mackenzie?" she countered.

A flicker of respect entered the boy's eyes. "She's at the end of the block," and he pointed at a brownstone with white flowers in the window. "She should be there now."

"Look," and Lola tore a twenty-dollar bill in half. "There's nowhere to park except right in front of that hydrant over there. I'm going to be ten, fifteen minutes tops. If you watch the car for me, I'll give you the other half of this when I come down. Deal?"

And with that negotiation nicely taken care of, Lola parked the Jeep, engaged the car alarm, and then climbed the short flight of stone stairs to number 21½. She pressed the button underneath the name Mackenzie, and said, "It's Lola St. James."

Audrey waited for the arrival of her visitor with tight lips, fuming beneath her breath as Lola climbed the two flights of stairs to her apartment. The nerve, the absolute nerve of the woman, coming here to see her. Well, she was ready for her. If Lola St. James thought for even one second that she was going to agree to the prospect of sharing Chaz Kelly with her, she would soon discover the kind of woman that she was dealing with.

Lola gave the weathered door a sharp knock and waited with calm eyes and face as the security chain was removed and the locks opened.

Audrey pulled back the door and for an instant the surprise showed in her eyes. So Lola St. James *was* beautiful. Audrey's glance took in the high sculpted cheekbones, the soft doe eyes exactly the right distance apart, the beautifully rounded nose, and the generous bow-shaped mouth. Heat rose to shimmer in her eyes. Lola was more than just merely beautiful, Audrey allowed grudgingly. The woman was simply drop-dead gorgeous.

Audrey blocked the opening to the small apartment with her body and gave no indication that she was about to invite her visitor in.

"I have things to do today," she said with a hard little note in her voice. "So whatever it was you wanted to say, you can say it right here."

Lola smiled at the other woman, and her analytical glance took in the well-worn shoes, the dress that had probably seen better days. The thirty-dollar watch on Audrey's hand.

"I think you'll want to hear what I have to say. And I have no intention of having this sort of conversation with you here in the hallway."

Audrey's eyes hardened. "Well, you can just go back the way you came then." And she moved to close the door.

Lola pressed against the wood with a hand. If she had to get tough with this woman, she was more than willing to, but first she would be nice.

"I think it would be wise of you to hear me out. What I want to speak to you about might very well change your entire life." She paused for effect and then continued. "You can turn me down, of course, but if I were in your shoes," and she made sure that she looked at the other woman's shoes before she went on, "I would at least think very carefully about my offer before doing so."

Audrey sniffed. "I couldn't care less about what you

might have to say." And she prepared to shut the door yet again.

Lola's left eyebrow tilted. "Even if it could take you out of this place? Give you the kind of life you deserve?"

Audrey pulled the door back by just a bit. "What do you mean, *take me out of this place*? I thought you wanted to talk to me about Chaz."

"I'll explain inside." And Lola gave the other woman a hard-as-nails look.

Audrey stepped away from the door with a barely civil, "Come in then. But I can only spare about five minutes. So whatever you want to say, you'd better make it quick."

"What I have to say," Lola said, stepping inside the crowded little apartment, "will take at least fifteen minutes."

Lola went across to a soft old sofa, sat, and then plunged into the discussion without further preamble.

"I want you to stop seeing Chaz," she said, snapping open her briefcase.

Audrey's mouth hung open for half an instant and then a tumult of angry words flowed.

Lola held up an imperious hand. "Look, I don't have the time for this. Either you're going to listen to me or you're not. It's your choice." Lola's calm expression belied the anger that was bubbling just beneath the surface. Anger not with Audrey but with Chaz. It was still completely unclear to her how he could actually prefer such a woman. Was he deranged? Or just mentally incompetent? Surely it was as plain as day that Audrey Mackenzie was nothing more than a coldhearted schemer who would probably treat him a lot worse than his first wife ever had.

Audrey settled herself in a facing chair and with a very stiff face said, "Go ahead."

Lola nodded. "Right. Now let's get down to business. Here's my proposal. For reasons of my own, which I will not go into, I want you to agree to break things off with Chaz, and," she directed a steely gaze Audrey's way as the other woman tried to interrupt yet again, "you are to have no contact whatsoever with him for a period of a year. In exchange for this, my attorney will deposit a sum of six thousand dollars each month into your account." She held up a hand to indicate that she was not yet finished. "He will also make certain that you meet the right producers and studio heads out there in Hollywood."

Audrey's mouth sagged again. "Hollywood?" she stammered.

Lola gave her a bland look. "Aren't you interested in becoming an actress? You are. Right," and she continued as though there was nothing more to say about it. "But if you break this agreement and attempt to contact him in any way during the next twelve months, the payments will end and all previous monies paid will be repaid to me."

Audrey crossed her legs before her. "Seventy-two thousand dollars stretched over twelve months. And at the end of that I can see Chaz again? Is that it?"

Lola nodded. "That's it."

"Well, for that amount of inconvenience, not to mention the emotional anguish I'll be going through, I want three hundred thousand dollars." And she adjusted the hemline of the frock about her knees. "Take it or leave it."

Lola closed her briefcase and prepared to stand. "My offer is not negotiable. Either you accept my terms right now or you live here and manage the best way you can. No money. No Hollywood. No Chaz."

Audrey blinked rapidly. She had felt certain that Lola St. James would give in to her. It was as plain as day that she had some sort of a genuine romantic interest in Chaz. But it would seem that she had underestimated her.

"I might not get the money," Audrey ventured after a moment's thought, "but I will get Chaz. It's me that he wants, and don't forget it. Besides, all I have to do is tell him about our little talk, and . . . Well I'm sure you can imagine the rest of it."

Lola's eyes narrowed to blistering slits. "You mention even one word of this, my dear, and I will destroy you." She tapped her case. "I have your personal romantic and credit history right here. Don't force me to use it."

And at Audrey's stunned look she said, "So are we in agreement? Twelve months. Seventy-two thousand dollars."

Later that evening, with the warmth of the day still in the curl of wind that raced through the treetops, Chaz walked slowly up the gravel drive toward the main house. He was tired, but it was the good kind of tiredness that came after a very productive day of work. Together with two of his best workers he had walked the entire property, taking meticulous pictures of the rolling grounds. The property as a whole was in pretty good shape, but there were a few spots that would need regrooming before he could get to work on the real job of redesigning the landscape with bushes and other shrubs, a nice little serenity enclosure with comfortable seats and a crystal-clear brook. The Jacuzzi would be the last thing he worked on. The entire job would probably take the better part of a year, but when he was through with the place, it would be a work of art. The best single advertisement for his business that he had yet done. There was only one problem, though, as far as he could see. And that problem came in a curvy and possibly vindictive little package. If he didn't find a way to adequately manage Lola St. James, all of his hard work would be for naught. He would get the million dollars they had agreed upon, of course, but none of the necessary recommendations that were so important to building his business. And of course if she really wanted to be vindictive, she had the connections and the power to completely ruin him.

He rang the front doorbell with the beginnings of a frown between his eyes and stood back to wait at the sound of footsteps. He looked down at his sweat-stained T-shirt and wondered for a moment if he should have stopped to change before coming up to the house.

The door opened and Chaz looked down into the smiling face of Mrs. Lewis.

"Well, hello," she said. And Chaz wondered why it was that she seemed to be so very pleased to see him.

He returned the woman's smile and said in a very

deep voice, "I just stopped by to get Jamie. I hope he didn't give you any trouble."

Annie pulled Chaz through the doorway with a very warm, "He's been a little angel." This fact was something that worried her severely, but she neglected to mention this as she ushered Chaz into the elegantly furnished foyer.

Chaz smoothed a hand down the front of his shirt. "I'll just wait here while you grab him," he said, and he laughed. "A full day of work equals a full day of sweat. And I wouldn't want to track mud and grime all over your clean floors."

Annie made a clucking sound with her tongue. "Nonsense. You must stay for dinner. We're having barbecued chicken, corn on the cob, scalloped potatoes, black-eyed pea soup, and my specialty."

"What's that?" Chaz grinned. The laundry list of mouthwatering foods brought a rumble to his stomach and he was really tempted to stay, just for a little while.

Annie balanced her hands on her ample hips. "Have you ever had watermelon and pineapple cider?"

Chaz shook his head. "Never."

"Well then," Annie beamed, "you have to stay."

And that, as far as she was concerned, was that. She led the way down into the spacious family room, her brain churning all the way. It was very clear now why it was that Lola liked this man. There was something about him. A charm. A genuineness. But Annie could also see that there was deep hurt there, too. Deep hurt.

A secretive little smile flashed in her eyes for a moment. But that was where Lola would come in. Her sweet Lola would love all of the hurt away. Of that Annie was absolutely certain.

Chaz followed the housekeeper, very conscious of the fact that his big rubber-soled boots were leaving a trail of very clear dirt marks across the beautiful cream-colored floor. As they got closer, the sound of melodious feminine laughter drifted up the stairs to meet him. Chaz hesitated for just an instant. Irrationally, he had been hoping that Lola would not be there. But it would seem that the fates were not to be so kind.

He heard his son laugh next and then Lola admonish gently, "Not a chance, young man. Down that snake you go."

Chaz stepped into the family room, and the clump of his boots raised Lola's head. She was curled up on the carpet, with one arm resting on a giant throw cushion.

"Oh, you're here," she said, and she smiled at him in a manner that brought a glint of humor to Chaz's eyes. His lips curled by just a bit. Yes. She was up to something else.

His voice rumbled in his chest. "Good evening."

"Hi, Dad," Jamie said, and then he resumed his contemplation of the Snakes and Ladders board game.

Chaz exchanged a grin with his son. "Hi yourself."

"Come in and sit," Lola beckoned, and she patted a spot close to where she was sitting.

When he was comfortably seated, Lola handed him the dice. "Let's see if you can beat this little boy. He's won almost every game we've played so far."

"I beat Mrs. Lewis, too, Dad." And the little boy chortled. "And I've never even played this game before."

Chaz took the dice. "Well, let's see if you can beat me."

And for the next hour there was laughter, mock threats, and more laughter. And, as they switched from one board game to the next, Chaz caught himself staring at Lola on more than one occasion. She seemed so warm and kind, and sweet. Surely this was not the real woman? The Lola St. James who ran people out of business? Who took away other women's men? His brow wrinkled at the thought. Could he have been wrong about her?

Lola laughed heartily as Chaz's game piece landed on one of her properties.

"Pay up," she said, and she stretched a hand with grasping fingers in his direction.

Chaz pretended to grumble, much to his son's amusement, as he handed over his final five hundred dollars. And game after game continued in much this manner until Annie bustled in to say, "Dinner."

Chapter Seventeen

Chaz walked home with a full stomach and a strangely happy feeling. It had been a nice evening. And, surprisingly enough, he had really enjoyed the time spent with Lola. He had caught himself laughing heartily from time to time at her irreverent wit and had been genuinely impressed by how well she seemed to relate to Jamie. The woman was a constant bundle of surprises. That was certain. But he liked her. It was hard for him to admit it, given all of the negative things he had thought about her, but it was true. She was hard not to like, and maybe that was part of the unusual power she had over men.

He looked down at his son now and tapped him affectionately behind the head.

"So you had a good time today?"

Jamie nodded. "Miss St. James said that I can come back anytime I like."

Chaz nodded. "That was nice of her, but we don't want to wear out our welcome. Right?" And he reached down to pull his cell phone from off his belt as it began to ring. The number scrolled slowly across the face, and he snapped the phone open to say, "Audrey."

• • •

Lola stood at the front door and watched them until they had both rounded the little curve in the drive; then she went back indoors and began helping Annie clear up. She carted the dishes out to the kitchen and spent several moments over the open garbage can, scraping each plate free of the remnants of the very delicious meal. She smiled at her housekeeper as the woman came through the door.

"You know, Annie," she began, "I really don't know what I would do without you."

Annie pursed her lips in a pleased manner. "I don't plan on leaving you anytime soon. So you won't have to do without me." She opened the dishwasher and began to load it. "What has me worried, though," she said after stacking plates into neat little rows, "is that little boy. I think he's planning something."

Lola scraped another dish and bit the corner of her bottom lip. Annie wouldn't be amused at all if she suddenly broke into gales of uncontrollable laughter.

"Yes," she allowed, "he was unusually good today. But maybe he was just having a good day."

Annie made a disbelieving sound. "That one? A good day? I'm sure he's never had one of those. He's up to something. Believe me. And when I find out what it is, I promise you I will take a slipper to his behind."

Lola chuckled and for that she earned a sharp glance from Annie.

"You won't think it's so funny when we find out what it is."

Lola handed over the final dish and then came across

to wrap a warm arm about Annie's middle.

"I took care of everything today."

Annie shot her a quick look. "The girl?"

Lola nodded. "Uhm-hmm. And a few other things, too. And, believe me, I don't feel guilty at all about getting rid of that woman. She's no good at all for Chaz. Besides, she doesn't love him."

"And you love him?" Annie asked carefully.

Lola turned on the tap and used the momentary distraction of water flowing to think. She had loved him once, and no matter what anyone had to say about it, her feelings for him then were real. But what did she really feel about him now? She had long since given up on any juvenile desire to pay him back for that long-ago incident.

"You know you have to treat him gently. I don't think he trusts easily. Not women anyway."

Lola turned off the water, dried her hands. "I know," she said, and she deliberately avoided answering Annie's earlier question about love. She wanted Chaz, more than she had ever wanted anyone or anything. But what did that mean?

"And he really doesn't trust women like me."

Annie loaded the final dish, closed the dishwasher, and turned the knob to wash.

"Well, you always knew that," she said. "What you have to do is make him see you. The real you." Annie gave her a motherly tap on the behind. "You understand what I mean?"

Lola smiled. Yes, she understood very well what Annie meant. It was time to pull out the big guns. It was time to blow his mind with sex.

Chapter Eighteen

The grounds of the property were a hotbed of activity. There were several pieces of large equipment, including two trucks, a front-end loader, and a cement mixer. Men walked back and forth carrying long planks, flowerpots, and pieces of bushy shrubbery.

Chaz Kelly stood in the midst of this, directing the activities of one of the trucks.

"Come on back. Come on back. Good. Good."

He shielded his eyes against the bright sunshine and beckoned the driver closer.

"Come on. You're all right."

The truck came to a shuddering stop at the lip of a small gravel pit and Chaz banged the side and bellowed, "Right! That's it!"

He stood back and watched as the first truck emptied more gravel into the half-full pit. He took a swig of water from the bottle strapped to his hip, wiped his forehead with the back of an arm. It was a scorching hot day, the kind that would send most people hustling for the shade. But the heat didn't really bother him at all. He loved the summer. In fact, if it were completely up to him, he might move to some place in the world where there was summer all the time. Some place like Barbados. Hawaii. Bermuda. And maybe he would now that Audrey was out of the picture. He was surprised at how little he felt about the entire matter. And he wasn't sorry, either, that she had chosen to break the relationship between them via a phone call. Had she decided to do it in person, there would have been explanations and tears and God only knew what else. Her decision had taken him a little by surprise, of course. But after he had wished her well and then hung up the phone he had realized that the feeling in him had not been anger or disappointment or even sorrow. It had been relief.

His brow wrinkled at the thought and he took another swallow of water. He knew exactly why he was relieved, of course. For months he had tried to ignore his gut. Had tried to tell himself that Audrey was the woman he should marry. But, deep down, he had always known that it would come to this. And the plain and simple reason for that deeply unsettled feeling within him was that he didn't love her. Couldn't love her. In fact, he didn't think that he would ever be able to love again. Because in order to love, first there had to be trust. And that was something he couldn't give again. Wouldn't give again.

The truck finished dumping its load and Chaz waved the driver forward. It was just about lunchtime. He usually ate with his crew, but today he would return to the house, down another portion of cold medicine, and then fix himself something quick.

Lola folded the white linen napkin with quick hands and placed it next to the shiny silver cutlery. Then she

walked back into the kitchen and bent to remove a tray
of freshly warmed rolls from the oven. She dumped
these into a pretty serving basket and clattered out to the
table again, taking particular care not to slip on the tiles
in her three-inch heels. She placed the basket in the center of the table and then went back in again for the baked
chicken and a large dish of greens garnished with sweet
onions and shallots. She spent a few minutes more ar-
ranging a pitcher of water and an ice bucket filled with
thick chunks of ice; then she went into the bathroom to
take a shower.

Chaz pushed open the front door, threw his keys
onto the table by the door, and made a beeline for the
bathroom. The cold medicine he had been taking for
the past several days was really doing a good job. It had
managed to just about knock the cold out of him entirely. In fact, he felt perfectly fine today. He was only
taking the medicine now as a just-in-case measure.
Colds were often sneaky things, and he couldn't afford
to suddenly come down sick. Not now.

He pushed the bathroom door and almost tripped
over a red lace bra.

"Audrey," he muttered, and he bent to disentangle
the garment from the tip of his boot.

The sound of the shower curtain being drawn open
brought him out of his bend.

"Jesus."

The single emphatic declaration reverberated in the
small room, and in reply to it, Lola uttered a very
pleased, "Amen." Then, with a wet and shapely arm
extended, she said nicely, "Would you pass me a towel,
please?"

Chaz reached blindly for the towel closest to him and then thrust it at her.

"What are you doing in my bathroom?" he asked when it became clear that she was going to dry herself before him.

Lola lifted a thick, well-shaped leg to rest on the lip of the bathtub, and then bent, so that a dusky dark-nippled breast rested on the curve of her thigh. She ran the thick towel along the inner curve of her leg and said in a reasonable manner, "I'm just taking a shower. I didn't think you'd mind."

The hand gripping the red lace bra tightened into a fist and a cord of muscle flexed in one arm.

"Ms. St. James—" he began.

But she interrupted him with a gentle admonishment.

"I thought we were beyond all that formality now?"

Chaz cleared his throat. He knew that he should really turn around and leave Lola St. James to complete her business in the bathroom, but Jesus, he just couldn't seem to stop staring. Her body was perfect. No less than a work of art. It was dark and thick and curvy and he was completely certain that should he put his tongue there, the soft point between her thighs would be sweet to the taste. . . .

"What . . . was that?" he asked in a slightly distracted manner. And he cleared the dryness from his throat with a rumbling cough against the palm of his hand.

Lola's voice was like soft velvet, and the hairs at the base of his spine twitched in reply.

"I was asking you to dry my back. Could you . . . please?"

Chaz's eyes followed the progress of the towel as it roved up a leg to the curve of her waist and then across her tight abdomen to gently kiss the dark center of a soft breast. His knees trembled and he drew in a harsh breath. This was not happening. He couldn't be losing his control over the simple sight of a woman. God almighty. Not since he was a young and callow teenage boy had he felt such . . . bare unbridled *lust*. In another time, another place, he would have dragged that slip of a towel away from her, pressed her up against the wet walls, and . . .

"Let me have the towel," he said, a gruff note in his voice. He knew exactly what had to be done. If he didn't prove to her right away that she couldn't use her body to manipulate him, she would have him eating out of her hand and following her around just like the legions of heartsick men he had heard about.

He took the towel from her outstretched hand and gritted his teeth. He had done difficult things in his life. Many of them, to be exact. So this would be no different. What did it matter if her skin had the feel of warm silk? It was just skin, after all. Ordinary skin. There was nothing, absolutely nothing, special about it.

He passed the towel quickly across her shoulder blades and did his best not to inhale the sweet fragrance of her hair.

"Lower," Lola husked softly. And, in a robotic manner, Chaz moved the towel down the run of her back. He fully realized that he was no longer in control of what was happening. But he didn't care. This woman had come after him. He had tried to do the honorable thing. Had tried to tell her up front that he could never be genuinely interested in her. But it hadn't done any good. Now here she was standing stark naked before him, tempting him with her body. What did she think he was made of? Steel? He was just a man after all, so she couldn't complain if he gave her exactly what it was she was begging him for.

Lola arched her back in a feline stretch as the towel made its way slowly down the length of her back. The round of her buttocks touched the fabric of his pants, and she rubbed against him in a provocative little movement. She felt his indrawn breath and then she was suddenly no longer in control. His hands closed about her waist and he lifted her from the hollow of the bathtub. The towel fell between them as they wrestled for balance, bare limbs thrown across stonewashed jeans.

Lola's heart shuddered in her breast as his head dipped toward her. She had waited so long for this. So very long. Now, the wait was over and finally, finally, she would know the feel of his lips.

She waited with a pocket of warm breath in her throat, her skin at once hot and cold. But his mouth missed hers entirely, and, before she could wonder at the inaccuracy of his aim, settled instead on the crest of a chocolate-smoothed nipple. He drew the soft center into the warmth of his mouth and suckled so strongly that Lola, caught by a swarm of intense feelings, cried out.

Chaz moved his mouth against her in a pulling rhythm and Lola's toes curled in reply. Unintelligible sound welled up in the back of her throat as he removed his mouth to ask, "Is this what you want? Huh?

Or is this it?" And the flat of his hand smoothed the run of her abdomen and then dipped below her navel to stroke and then part the heated flesh beneath. Firmly, skillfully, he located the short nub of flesh and then with the tip of a calloused thumb, he massaged. Lola groaned her pleasure against his neck, and Chaz shuddered in response. He had thought that this level of feeling was behind him, but this woman, this woman was like no other.

"Wait," he said huskily as Lola pulled at his shirt. It had been such a very long time for him that he was totally unprepared for this level of intimacy.

"No," Lola muttered peevishly, and she bit the warm column of flesh at the junction of his neck and shoulder.

Chaz moved her slowly away from him and took advantage of this moment of sanity to draw several ragged breaths.

"We can't. Not right now."

Lola lifted her head. Good God, in her haste to get him out of his clothes, she had totally forgotten about the boy.

"Oh. Jamie," she said now.

Chaz bent to retrieve the towel and wrapped it firmly about her.

"Not Jamie. He's at camp today."

"Then what?" And she wrapped both arms about his waist and refused to let him go even when he made a halfhearted attempt to free himself.

Chaz debated for a minute whether or not to answer that question with the truth. A woman like Lola St. James would never understand the concept of celibacy.

Granted, it had not been entirely his idea, but he had not resisted the thought of it too hard. Sex with Audrey had never been an earth-shattering experience.

"It's been a long time for me, so I'm not prepared."

Lola smiled up at him. "How long? A week?"

Chaz's chest moved in a silent chuckle. "More like a year."

"A year? Come on. What about your . . . your friend?" And Lola stood on tiptoe to rub her nose against the tip of his, a move that startled Chaz into momentary silence.

"We're not together anymore," he said, and there was a note of finality in his voice. He had absolutely no intention of beginning a discussion with Lola St. James about his sex life. Especially when she was far too close to him and clothed in a much too short towel.

Lola stepped back a bit. She could sense that he was beginning to withdraw from her again, and she had to press home her advantage while she still had it. She had not expected him to respond to her so quickly and she certainly had not expected her off-the-charts response to him.

"I brought you lunch, by the way."

Chaz glanced at his watch. Damn. He had even forgotten that he was working today.

"I've got to get back. The men—"

"The men can give you just a half an hour more to eat, I'm sure. Besides, you can't do a full day of work on an empty stomach. Can you?"

Lola didn't wait for his response. Instead, she took him by the hand and led him into the dining room, where the table was set and the food laid out.

She pulled out a chair and ushered him into it with an authoritative, "Sit."

"You are probably one of the bossiest women I have ever met," Chaz said, sitting.

Lola ignored that and instead stretched a hand for his plate. She ladled spicy greens, a healthy serving of baked chicken, and a soft lunch roll onto the plate and then handed everything back.

Chaz accepted the plate without comment and tried not to watch her as she spread the towel wide and then tucked herself more securely into it.

He waited for her to seat herself.

"Can I start?"

Lola gave him a surprised glance. "Sure. Sure. Go ahead." She watched him dig into the food as she dished herself a small helping. This was so nice, having him sitting across from her. She had fantasized about this very thing for years, and now, through hard work and unexplainable fortune, here he was. Here *they* were.

She sampled a forkful of greens and bent her head so that he wouldn't notice the wistful expression in her eyes. It was so very silly how prominent in her mind and in her life she had let him become. Most grown women, if they were truthful, would admit to having at least one significant childhood crush, but after leaving high school they also left that juvenile infatuation behind. She, however, had allowed it to define her entire life. Crazy.

Chaz loaded his fork with chicken, some greens, and a soft hunk of bread.

"What?" he asked between chews.

Lola blinked at him. Had she spoken aloud?

"Ah . . . lemonade? Don't you want something to drink with that?"

Chaz picked up the jug, poured himself a glass. He gave her an inquiring glance before setting the pitcher back on the table.

Lola waved it away with a, "No, I'm fine."

Chaz took a swig from his glass. "You were saying that something was crazy?" Why it was he was attempting to make conversation with this woman, he didn't know. By all rights, he should be laying down the law about her breaking into his house . . . or at the very least, he should be letting her know that she couldn't just waltz in and out of his place whenever the mood took her. But, strangely, he felt no anger or outrage whatsoever. And, not only that, but he had also come to a decision. . . .

"I was just thinking about my high school days," Lola said, and she gave him a quick glance.

Chaz laughed. "High school? Not college?"

"No. High school. It's where everything began for me."

Chaz spooned another helping of greens into his plate, selected another leg of chicken.

"I'll bet you were one of those high achievers. Probably got A's in everything. Won all the popularity contests."

Lola wrinkled her nose. "Wrong. I wasn't popular at all. In fact," and she paused to pour herself a glass of water, "I was even what you might call . . . socially awkward."

"Socially awkward? You? I don't believe it."

"Well, believe it." Her eyes met his, and she said in a silky voice, "Even my date for the senior prom stood me up."

Chaz took another swallow of lemonade, began to wipe his mouth with the back of his hand, and then remembered the napkin on his lap. He crumpled it in his hand, patted his mouth for a few seconds, and then said, "Well, kids do foolish things. But I'm sure he's kicking himself today."

Lola itched to ask him the question that had bothered her for so many years, but instead she said, "Have you had enough?"

"Umm," Chaz said, and he scraped back his chair and stood. "Listen. I've been thinking . . . but this isn't the right time to discuss this."

Lola's mouth went dry. "Tonight then? I could ask Annie to baby-sit Jamie." She didn't want to appear too eager, but she had a feeling, a good feeling.

"You're sure Mrs. Lewis won't mind?"

Heat surged in Lola's cheeks. "Of course she won't mind. Annie loves that boy—I do, too." She added the last three words with some amount of haste. She didn't want Chaz to get the impression that she didn't care for children. She did. Most of the time.

He appeared to consider her for a moment and then, with a puzzling smile flickering behind his eyes, agreed. "OK. Tonight at eight then?"

Chapter Nineteen

The remainder of the day passed much too slowly for Lola's liking. She spent a bit of time on the phone talking to her lawyer and listened carefully to the arrangements that were currently under way to relocate Audrey Mackenzie to the West Coast. She approved the first deposit to Audrey's account, since it was clear that her rival had kept her side of the deal and broken off things with Chaz. Then she spent a little time chatting on the phone with Camille about the progress of things and laughing heartily at her friend's descriptions of what lovemaking was like with her elderly fiancé.

Just before five-thirty, she settled into a leisurely bubble bath of scented jasmine and allowed herself the luxury of a good long soak. She dried and creamed every inch of skin and then stood for a while at the window watching the trucks and other pieces of equipment roll down the drive and through the gates. When the grounds were quiet again, she walked across to her queen-size bed, stripped it bare, and replaced the old sheets with smooth satin. She lingered over the pillows, fluffing them so that they had just the right degree of softness. Then she went to her closet to choose a little black dress with a conservative neckline and a plunging back. She combed her hair into soft shoulder-length ringlets and then went to work on her face.

Annie popped into the bedroom as Lola applied the final pat of powder to her cheekbones.

"Everything all set?"

Lola turned with powder brush still in hand. "All ready to go. Don't worry, Annie. We'll have dinner, and then," she smiled, "things will follow their natural course."

The housekeeper made a little sound of disapproval. She still didn't agree with the way young people did things these days, it all seemed backward to her, but Lola was a grown woman well aware of what she was doing and more skilled than most in taking care of herself.

"You're sure you don't want me to stay for a little while? Just through the shrimp course?"

Lola stood. "If things go the way I think they will, we might not even make it through dinner." She gave a half twirl. "How's the dress look?"

Chaz pulled the cotton shirt open and swore softly as two buttons bounced to the floor and went rolling in opposite directions. Damn it. Damn it. Damn it. This was all he needed now. Loose buttons, hiding only God knew where. And why hadn't he noticed that there was a stain on the cuff of one sleeve? He would have to try to sponge that out, iron it again, and then locate the buttons.

He raised his voice and hollered, "Jamie! Jamie!"

The boy came running after several minutes of shouting.

"Didn't you hear me calling you?" Chaz waved away his son's explanations. "Get me the mail from the box, and . . . " he gave the boy a flickering glance, "change that shirt before Mrs. Lewis gets here. It's filthy. What have you been doing? Rolling around in the mud?"

Chaz went off to the bathroom muttering beneath his breath about single fatherhood. Everyone always had a truckload of advice for single mothers, but what about the good family-oriented men out there who were trying to raise children alone? There were few magazine articles about them.

He pushed open the bathroom door and then picked his way across the floor, bending to throw clothes and towels across an arm as he went. The boy was turning into a very sloppy young man. Chaz would have to sit him down one day very soon and explain the importance of—

"Dad. Dad." His son's voice cut through his thoughts.

He turned with arms full of clothes, momentarily concerned.

"I'm in the bathroom."

Jamie came barreling through the door, and Chaz, genuinely worried now, dropped the clothes.

"Breathe, boy. Breathe."

"The letter—"

"Yes. You got the mail," he said with some degree of patience.

The boy took a large gulp of air. "Remember the letter I sent to . . . to Mom out in California?"

Chaz's brow wrinkled. It broke his heart every time that woman he had married hurt his child callously. He struggled for the right thing to say and finally reached out to drag the boy close. "It's all right, son," he began. "You know how busy your mother usually is. I'm sure one of these days she'll be able to—"

The boy beamed at him. "This time she's coming, Dad," he said, and he waved the torn envelope at his father.

"What do you mean, she's coming?" And Chaz took the letter from the boy's outstretched hand. He scanned it quickly, rubbed a hand across his jaw, and then read it again. Well, if that didn't just beat everything. She was getting divorced again, so she was coming to the East Coast for some rest. She wanted to spend a little time with her son and wondered if they could arrange something?

He ran a hand across his jaw again. Jesus. Now this was a bolt out of the blue. Never once in all of the years since Jamie had been born had she ever shown a single bit of interest in seeing the child. Not even the occasional birthday card or Christmas card had she thought to send. She had made it quite clear that she had no interest whatsoever in being a part of the boy's life. Hell, the child wouldn't even know what she looked like if he hadn't kept an old picture of her around.

Jamie was jumping up and down. "Can she come, Dad? Can she come?"

Chaz looked down at his son's eager face. He would have to think about this. He would have to think about this really carefully. It wasn't that he didn't want Jamie to know his mother. Or that he was afraid that she might try to take the boy away from him. He just did not trust his ex-wife's motives one single bit. He was certain that she was after something. But what that something was—that was the million-dollar question.

"We'll see, Jamie. We'll see." And at the boy's slightly downcast face said, "I'll write to her. OK? Now help me pick up these things; then go get me the rest of the mail."

"I think out by the pool would be great. Let me take these out." Lola rested a nicely arranged dish of jumbo shrimp on the food cart and then wheeled it toward the French doors. A soft gust of evening breeze blew her curls up over her ears and she patted at her hair with a hand. It was a gorgeous night. Not too warm but not cool enough for a sweater. The sky was a smooth indigo with tiny pinpoints of light. And the sweet fragrance of summer shimmered in the air.

Lola sucked in a breath and then turned back to Annie with sparkling eyes.

"You know, I think you're right."

Annie, just behind, pushing a rattling trolley of drinks, said, "Right about what?"

Lola secured the food cart by stepping on the wheel brake.

"Maybe I should have told Chaz from the start who I am. It just seems silly now keeping it a secret."

"Well," and Annie pushed the trolley right next to the first cart, "that's exactly what I've been saying all along. I can't understand why you kept it a secret in the first place."

"You wouldn't understand."

Annie placed several chunks of ice into a glass and handed it to Lola.

"You'd be surprised to know how much I do understand."

Lola gave her a startled look. "What do you mean?"

Annie smiled and gave Lola a motherly pat on the arm. "One of these days I'll tell you. But," and she got a look of bright excitement in her eyes, "you've got more important things to pay attention to. It's," she shot a quick look at her watch, "almost eight o'clock. And I have to get over yonder to see to the demon child."

Lola laughed at that and was still chuckling a few minutes later as she ushered Chaz out to the large pool deck.

He appeared a little uncomfortable and Lola wracked her brains for something to say that would put him at ease. She hadn't really noticed it before, but he was definitely shy around her. Now what that meant exactly, she wasn't sure. Especially given their heated exchange in the bathroom earlier in the day. But she aimed to work every ounce of discomfort out of him, one way or the other.

Chaz dragged out a chair for her and then seated himself. He was dressed in a long-sleeved navy blue shirt buttoned down at the neck and a matching pair of navy slacks. Lola's discerning eye ran over him. He looked nice enough, but the clothes had a well-worn look to them. Not shabby, exactly, but well on the way to being just that.

"Is your neck sore?" The words seemed to hang in the air for a moment and Lola's teeth closed on the side of her tongue. Stupid. Stupid. Stupid move. She shouldn't have said that. She had wanted to play it cool even though she'd damn near jumped his bones earlier in the day. Still, she wanted to keep him guessing—just in case his reason for wanting to meet with her was not what she thought it might be.

Chaz rubbed a hand across the back of his neck. Perceptive woman. Most days, he ended up with a muscle ache of one kind or another. And today it was his neck and the butterfly muscle in his back. But he didn't want to talk about his aching muscles. What he did want to discuss was . . .

He cleared his throat and Lola forestalled him with an offer of shrimp. He accepted one of the nicely cooked jumbos, took a minute to dip the succulent head in spicy red sauce, and then got down to the heart of the matter.

"I'm sure you must be wondering what this is all about."

Lola spread her fingers. She was certain that she knew what it was all about, but she let him continue.

He scratched the back of his neck, and proceeded to look so very uncomfortable about the whole thing, that Lola almost broke down and helped him out.

"I've been doing some thinking . . . about . . . well . . . about us."

"Um-hmm." Lola selected a shrimp, dipped it in sauce, bit down. The flavor was hot and sweet on the tongue.

"I know you're a direct woman, and I'm just an old-fashioned country boy."

A smile bloomed in Lola's eyes and she leaned over the bowl of dip. She just itched to remind him that he

had been born in the District of Columbia, not somewhere deep in the sticks. But she held on to her tongue
and instead gave him another considered, "Um."

Chaz cracked the knuckles on both of his hands.
"What I'm trying to say, and probably not well, is that
I'd like to take you up on your offer."

She leaned forward to open the soup tureen. "My
offer? You mean the affair?"

Chaz nodded and he gave a rueful laugh. "If you
were just pulling my leg a few days ago, I'm gonna feel
like a real fool, because—"

"Oh, I was very serious," Lola interrupted. And she
tried her best to keep her thumping heart under proper
control. It would not do at all for him to see how very,
very excited she was. It would give him too much
power over her, and she always had to have the upper
hand. Always.

Chaz smiled and he relaxed visibly. "Well, that's a
load off my mind."

Lola dished a bowl of sweet potato soup and handed
it to him with a rock-steady hand.

"Did you think I had changed my mind? Even after
this afternoon?"

Chaz laughed. "God. You don't mince words at all,
do you?"

Lola crossed her legs. "Not when it's something I
really want. Wine?" And she picked up a bottle of dark
red Bordeaux.

Chaz extended a fluted wineglass and wondered for
a brief minute as the glass was filled whether or not he
had actually lost his mind. How could he be seated
here by her pool, talking to her about this? He had

completely sworn off all women like Lola St. James. This was ridiculous. All she could possibly offer him was sex. Sex.

He took a sip of the wine, and the smooth full-bodied feel of it warmed the back of his throat. He made a low sound of pleasure. A purely sexual relationship wasn't such a bad thing. There were many good things about it. Many good things.

"I think we should discuss a few ground rules." She lifted an eyebrow. "If that's OK with you?"

Chaz swirled the wine in his glass, took another pleasing swallow. "Ground rules are good."

Lola nodded. "First," and she stopped to give this one a bit more thought, "we have to agree from the out-set that the sex can take place at any time . . . or place." She lifted a hand as he drew breath to interrupt. "What I mean by that is . . . say it's one o'clock in the morn-ing and I'm feeling a little . . . shall we say randy? I have the right to pick up the phone, call you up. And of course, you have to come."

"Well, there's Jamie," Chaz began.

Lola took a swallow of her wine. "Of course. I've thought about that. These late-night booty calls can only happen if Annie is available to sit. It can work," she said at the expression on his face.

He shook his head. "I'm a very private kind of guy, you know. And with all of that running back and forth, Mrs. Lewis would definitely know what was going on."

"Hmm," Lola said. Dealing with old-fashioned men was such a problem in this very modern age. "OK. How about this? Annie baby-sits for you a few nights a week from eight to midnight. That way, we keep whatever we're doing completely private." It would also cut down on the sex, but that couldn't be helped.

"Not bad," Chaz agreed. "But what about poor Mrs. Lewis? We'll be working her to death."

Lola waved this away. "I'll help her during the day. When she has a really heavy workload, I do that anyway. Trust me, I worry more about her than anyone else."

It was his turn to give her a contemplative, "Umm." He tapped the side of his jaw with an index finger. "I think we should make something completely clear, too . . . just so there's no, ah, confusion later."

"Go ahead," Lola said in a businesslike manner. Whatever he had to say now she would probably agree with. If later she found that it wasn't to her liking, she would just change it.

His eyes met hers and there was a hard little light there.

"No love."

Lola took another swallow of wine before saying, "What?"

"I think it should be completely clear now that this whole love thing is not part of the deal. Not part of the equation. I know this probably doesn't apply to you, but you know how sometimes sex," he paused to select another shrimp, "really, really good sex, can get people confused about love and marriage and that sort of thing. I just don't want us to get caught up in all that nonsense. This thing between us is going to be strictly sexual."

"Right." And Lola clinked her glass against his. "Strictly sexual. And," she added, holding up a finger, "there'll be no strings if one of us thinks it's time to walk away."

Chaz chomped on the shrimp. "Of course." He smiled at her. Now why couldn't all women be this sensible about sex? They always managed to develop some sort of an emotional attachment to the man they were sleeping with. This was exactly the kind of relationship he needed right now. And when it was over, they would both walk away. No one hurt. No one disillusioned. It was perfect. If he'd been thinking at all, he would have gotten himself this kind of woman ages ago.

Lola pointed at his bowl of soup. "Let's get started on the food before it gets cold."

"No more ground rules?" And he smiled in a manner that made Lola go warm all over.

"Well," she said, "I have a very developed sex drive, so I'm going to want this as many times a week as you can manage."

Chaz sampled a spoonful of chunky soup. "I don't think you'll have a problem there." He lifted his head. "This is good soup."

Lola gave him another, "Umm" and then said, "It's Annie's favorite recipe."

"The woman is a marvel. And I'll tell her that when I see her."

"There's something else."

"Shoot," Chaz said with a very agreeable note in his voice.

"We should be free to go out with anyone we like during the course of this arrangement."

Chaz gave her a look of genuine admiration. "Jesus. What a woman. Are you sure you don't have an Adam's apple under that neckline?"

Lola's eyes flickered with amusement. "I'm all

woman, baby. And you'll find that out soon enough."

Chaz threw back his head, laughed, and the sound of it brought shimmering memories to Lola's eyes. God, it had been such a long while. Why hadn't she decided to find him sooner? Why had she let him do without her for so long?

"You know," she said, "I think this relationship is going to be an excellent thing for both of us."

"As long as we're both discreet, there shouldn't be a problem. You know," and he leaned both elbows on the table, "since we met that first day, I've had the feeling that I can really talk to you."

Lola poured some more wine. "I guess that's why you were giving me the evil eye *and* the cold shoulder?"

Chaz reached out to take her hand in his. He rubbed the soft skin of her palm with the blunt of his thumbnail.

"Sorry about that. I had heard things . . . no excuse, I know. But I had gotten it into my head that . . ." He thought about how best to put it. "Well, that you were a certain kind of woman."

"Not one that you would have any time for."

He agreed with a brief nod. "Not one that I would have any time for."

Lola lifted an eyebrow. "And you changed your mind . . . why?" She felt the need to push him. To tease him. To shake him from the placid little comfort zone in which he had existed for so long.

"The truth?"

She nodded. "Always. We're grown-ups. Right?"

"You're an attractive woman. A beautiful woman. And that body of yours is genius itself."

Lola chuckled. "You're a superficial man, Chaz Kelly."

Chaz emptied his wineglass, poured himself another. "There comes a time in every man's life when a little superficiality will come into play. And believe me, after the kind of year I've had, that's exactly the sort of thing I need."

Lola tapped him on the hand with a beautifully manicured nail.

"A frank answer deserves a frank question." She rubbed the flesh of his palm with the flat of her own. "I really don't feel that hungry for food. So . . . are you ready to move this discussion upstairs?"

Chapter Twenty

"Now, let's see," and Lola tossed him a provocative little look. "Where should we start?"

Chaz took a look around the large bedroom suite. It was a well-appointed room, done in pleasing shades of cream and mauve, and even though he hardly ever noticed these things, he couldn't help admiring the plush beauty of the place.

He gave her half a smile and asked, "Would the bed be too conservative for you?"

Lola grinned. "Oh, do you think I'm a wild woman? Is that it?"

Her words brought the smile flickering in his eyes into full life. "Well, let's just say that I'd be really surprised if it turned out that you were ever the head of the local PTA."

Lola stepped out of a shoe and then shuffled off the other with the ball of her heel.

"Are you saying that you don't think I could be the head of the local PTA?"

Chaz sat on the bed. "I don't think I'd better answer that one. I have a feeling that this poor country boy may have blundered into some dangerous territory."

Lola propped both hands on her hips. "You, Mr. Kelly, have a whole lot to learn about me. But," and she moved a hand slowly up the inner swell of her thigh and then back down, "I'm very willing to teach you."

Chaz laughed. "Really?"

"Uhm-hmm."

He leaned back on his elbows, perfectly willing to let things unfold as they would. He had spent way too many years doing the right thing. Trying to think in the right way. But somehow, somewhere along the way, he had lost his true self. And now through this wild and very freaky woman, he would regain at least a little piece of the man he used to be. The good piece of the man he used to be.

He watched her through slitted eyes as she went about the room, busying herself with different things. Music. A little Luther turned down low. Lights. Soft pink and easy on the eyes. Butter . . . What?

He sat up. "Are we having more food?"

Lola trilled a silvery laugh. "In a manner of speaking. Take off your shirt. Slowly," she said as his fingers went immediately to pick at the buttons. She watched the long blunt-tipped fingers as they slid from one button to the next. Jesus, but she was going to enjoy this in so many different and unusual ways.

"Stop," she instructed as his hands went to the silver-headed belt buckle. "Pull your shirt open so I can see your chest."

"Bossy woman." But he did as she asked. "Now you," he said.

She smiled and asked, "What do you want to see first?" And for a brief moment, something about the way her lips tilted upward in that very saucy manner caused Chaz to struggle with elusive memory.

"I'll let you choose this time."

Lola reached behind her for the half zipper expertly hidden in the seams of the dress. She pulled and then rolled both shoulders out of the fabric. Gravity took the garment to her trim waist and she let it slide.

Chaz expelled a breath. God almighty she was hot. And she was touching herself now. Christ. It was too much. Too much for one man to bear. If she kept this up, he would have her down on the ground on the very spot on which she was now standing.

Lola rubbed the flat of her palm across the lacy bra. "Do you like?"

Chaz rumbled an affirmative and Lola responded by peeling back the lacy folds of one bra cup.

"And would you like to taste?"

"Yes."

She met his dark gaze and noticed the way in which the hunger leaped within him. A pleased smile lit in her eyes.

She walked slowly toward him with one broad, dusky nipple exposed, slab of paper-wrapped butter in one hand.

Chaz rose on his elbows. His mouth was beginning to water. Lord. This had never happened to him before. This hard, driving, searing need to spin her onto her back and fill her with his seed. Not even as a teenage boy, when his hormones were constantly in overdrive, had he ever felt like this.

Lola pushed him backward with a hand, climbed onto the bed so that she straddled each leg with a thick thigh.

"Tell me how much you want me," she said, and her eyes glittered at him with dark and seductive lights.

"I want you." His voice was hoarse, dry, a crack of sound that was totally alien even to his own ears.

"How much?" She brushed the blunt of his mouth with a nipple and then moved back out of reach when he attempted to take it.

"How much?"

"A lot." He cleared his throat. "Very much."

Sweat glistened on the curve of his brow and Lola longed to bend and remove the shine of it with her tongue, but she held on to the urge. All in good time. All in good time.

"OK." She smiled. "That will do for now." She peeled away the paper from the slab of butter and with great deliberation rubbed a smear of it onto the circle of her right nipple.

Chaz groaned, and Lola rubbed her groin against him and then leaned in to offer what he so obviously needed. His hands came up to splay across her back and he dragged her toward him. She resisted him for half a moment because she knew that it would be better that way, and then she gave way to his strength and allowed him to suckle.

His tongue slid over the creamy tip and then he pulled against her with such intensity, with such deliberation, that sweet heat pooled in the pit of her abdomen and she cried out for him, her words garbled, desperate.

"You like that?" It was his turn to ask, and Lola blinked eyelashes that had gone spiky.

"More than you'll ever know," she muttered heatedly.

Chaz took his time with her, moving with deliberate leisure from one nipple to the next, his tongue lavishing each swollen tip with elaborate attention. Lola held his head against her, straining to get him closer and closer still. Her legs wrapped tightly about his waist, and she lifted her rump to allow him to pull the rest of the dress from her. His hands moved over her stomach, dipped into the navel, slid underneath the band of elastic holding up her mesh underwear. She sucked in her cheeks as they went lower and lower still. Touching, stroking, caressing. Parting curls of hair, searching, seeking until finally he held her. His fingers were gentle yet firm as they moved slowly across the sensitive nub of flesh.

Lola bit the cheeks of her mouth. How much longer could she hold on? How much longer could she hold to this big, bad, bold role, when all she really wanted was to let the salty tears that were huddled in the back of her throat follow their natural course? She was a woman. His woman. This had always been so. This would always be so.

She sniffled and turned her face into the warm column of his neck. She couldn't crack now. She couldn't let him see what he was doing to her. But God, it was hard to hold on. It was so hard. . . .

Her fingernails bit into the skin of his back, and Chaz welcomed the feel of them. He was hot. She was hot. This was better than anything he had imagined. He wanted her. Had to have her. Now. Now.

He flipped her effortlessly so that she was staring up at him, her dark eyes filled with mystery and heat. He removed the mesh from her and then bent his head to taste. Lola held his head. Jesus. Sweet Jesus. She was going to pass out. It was too much. Too much.

His tongue wrapped around each lobe of flesh, stroking, thrusting, somehow finding all of those secret places that no one had ever thought to look for. Her legs lifted, gripped his shoulders. Broken sound drifted from her as his tongue began to thrust. She called out to him, once, twice, three times. Not caring what she said. Not caring at that moment who heard her.

"Chaz. . . ."

He knew what it was she needed even before the last letter of his name had passed her lips, but still he withheld himself. His tongue dipped and retreated. Dipped and retreated. A hot pink thing caught up in some primitive primordial dance of its own. She pulled at him, her fingers in his hair, on the sides of his face, raking across his shoulders. Her eyes were fierce now, desperate and wild.

"Now," she said, and her voice was thready steel.

"Not yet." His voice, husky, hoarse, in command.

But she couldn't wait any longer. Wouldn't wait any longer. She used her weight to turn him, pushed him backward when he would have risen, and then straddled him with big, thick thighs. Her legs were as strong as those of any man and she used them now to hold him still. She mounted him in one firm thrust of her hips and shuddered as waves of pleasure coursed the length of her spine. She heard him call out to the Almighty, and she gritted her teeth and began to move. His hands gripped each buttock, forcing her to match his rhythm. She leaned forward to offer him her bosom, and he took it, greedily. Her body moved over him in deep lunges, her hands gripping his shoulders, her back buckling and lengthening in a rapid, desperate rhythm. The bed creaked; the headboard rattled; the pictures on the walls shuddered. A vase crashed to the floor. He groaned something unintelligible, and Lola rode him harder still, ducking low against his body and raising her hips as high as she could get them. She closed her eyes and tried to block out all thought. But the words poured in on her nevertheless. This was impossible, improbable, unbelievable. It was too good. Too sweet. Too right. Jesus, God, and all the saints. But . . . what was happening? What was he doing? Was he . . . turning her? Why? Her eyes blinked open and fractured sound escaped:

"No . . . don't."

But he turned her nevertheless, positioning her legs about his waist, taking over where she had been forced to leave off. His thrusts were long and deep, and Lola arched her neck backward as involuntary spasms took her. She cried out for relief and sobbed salty tears when he bent her legs up around his neck and deepened the rhythm. Darkness splintered around the edges of her eyes, and for one confused moment she didn't understand. Couldn't understand. And then blissfully, without more than a whisper, the darkness took her.

Lola awoke to find a cool washcloth being pressed across her forehead. She blinked languorous eyes at him, wondering for an instant if this was just one of her wonderful waking dreams. He was lying over her, half of his face in shadow, beads of perspiration still peppering his brow. She touched one side of his face with a bemused finger and asked, "Are you real?"

He held the finger for a moment and then gently stroked her face with the cloth.

"You passed out."

"What?" Lola stuttered. Passed out? She had never passed out before in her life. And besides, if anyone was going to do any passing out here, it would definitely be him. She was a pistol in bed, after all. Everyone knew that she had never been bested. Could never be. And this was how she planned to get him. This was what she was going to use to make him love her. So how could she possibly do anything as ridiculous as pass out? It was just not in the cards.

She sniffed and then said in a superior manner, "I most certainly did not pass out."

Chaz removed the cloth, balled it in one hand, and then flung it onto the bedside table.

"Do you have any health concerns that I should know about?"

Lola's eyes widened. "Health concerns? What do you mean?"

"I mean, like a bad heart or a tendency to drop in a sudden dead faint . . . you know, that sort of thing."

"Listen to me, mister," and she attempted to gain better control of the situation by leaning on the bend of an elbow. "I am as fit as that proverbial old horse. And let me tell you, in the next go-round, *I'll* be the one asking all the questions."

He stroked the curve of one of her eyebrows. "I guess you can try. But, I have to warn you, I am made of much sterner stuff than that."

Lola pushed him onto his back. "Well, let's just give it a whirl then, huh?"

Chapter Twenty-one

Morning found Lola curled on her side, her legs drawn high up against her chest. She stretched slowly, turned to feel for him. And when her fingers closed on nothing but empty space, she blinked sleepy but well-satiated eyes open to greet the morning. She lay without moving, watching the red of the sun as it gradually showed itself above the treetops. Already there was birdsong in the air, and the whistle of wind in the leaves. She stretched again and allowed the memory of the night before to fold itself around her. What a night. What a crazy, freaky, absolutely satisfying night. She had known that they would be good together, but Lord almighty, good to the point of unconsciousness? That was really something that she'd never thought she'd ever experience. And although he had tried to be completely cool about it, she had known that it had been just as good for him. There was only one thing, though, that, now that she really thought about it, bothered the life out of her. In all of the time that they had spent together the night before, not once had he kissed her.

Her brows knit, and she pulled herself into a sitting position, propped two large pillows against the small of her back. She hadn't kissed him, either, but that had all been part of her strategy. But what had been *his* reason for not even trying to kiss her?

She turned the question over and over in her mind until finally the right idea struck her. And when Annie's expected knock sounded on her bedroom door, she called a very cheerful, "Come in!"

Surprise flashed across her face as the door opened and Camille poked her head around the lip.

"What are you doing here?"

Camille gave her a conspiratorial wink. "Ideas for wedding invitations. I've gotta get over to the printer's before ten." She dropped a cascade of cards to the floor and Lola uncurled from her comfortable spot, wrapped herself in a robe, and then went over to lend a hand.

Camille was down on her hands and knees, and Lola stilled her efforts with a hand.

"Take it easy, girl. What's the matter with you?"

Camille gathered a pile of cards, shoved them at her friend, and then broke: "He's useless. Useless, I'm telling you. He won't help me with anything." She sniffed mournfully. "I just don't know how he expects me to pull off a wedding, a whole wedding, in less than six months."

Lola gathered some more cards, carried her stash back to the bed.

"That less-than-six-months thing was your idea, Cam. I told you it wouldn't be enough time."

Camille plunked herself down on the large fourposter bed and appeared to notice the general disarray of the room for the very first time.

"What happened in here?" And then she gripped Lola's hand and said, "No."

Lola nodded, looking as pleased as punch. "Yes. But let's get through these invitations first."

Camille tossed the cards in her hands into the air. "Damn the invitations. I want details."

It was close to lunchtime, and Chaz half-expected her to appear with a tray of food for him. But as the minute hand ticked closer to the noon hour, he clomped to the kitchen in his work boots and began digging around in the back of a cupboard for tuna fish and pickles. He rested these on the kitchen counter and then went across to the bread bin to get a loaf of wheat bread. He pulled out a bowl and a fork, and then went to work on the tuna. His brow wrinkled into frown lines as he squeezed half a lemon over the fish, sprinkled some black pepper, added half a spoonful of mayonnaise. Contrary woman. She meant to keep him guessing. Well, he wouldn't play her game. She obviously wanted him to become dependent on her, but he had been taking care of himself for a long while now, so if she thought to manipulate him in this way, she was definitely barking up the wrong tree.

He slapped the fish onto a thick slice of bread, pulled open the fridge. OK. They had spent a good few hours together, an amazing few hours together, but it didn't mean anything. He could get along just fine without her. He slammed the fridge shut, and his breathing stilled for a moment at the sound of the doorbell. The tension that had begun to mount between his eyes was suddenly gone. *Now, that's more like it.* She was late, though;

didn't she know that most days he only took a half an hour for lunch?

He pulled back the door without checking. The man standing on the doorstep grinned at him in a friendly manner.

"Got your mail for you. I usually ring before leaving it in your box."

Chaz accepted the short stack and closed the door with the toe of his boot. Damn woman. He had a good mind to call her over right now for some more sex. It had been one of her rules after all. Sex at any time of the day or night.

He went back out to the kitchen, completed his sandwich, poured himself a tumbler of ice-cold water, and then returned to the dining room to sit. He chomped on the bread as he went through the mail. Bill. Bill. Junk. Another bill. God almighty but he was hungry for her. It was unnatural how much he wanted her. It had taken all of his strength this morning to get up and leave her lying there in bed. What was this strange power that she seemed to have over men?

His fingers paused as he waded through the stack of mail. A letter from the bank. His jaw clenched. Another rejection, no doubt. He finished his sandwich, swallowed half the tumbler of water, and then opened the green and white envelope. He scanned the first page of the document, then went back to the top of it to read again, carefully.

When he was through, he bowed his head against a clenched fist and said, "God. Thank you."

The loan. The last outstanding application he had

out there had gone through. It was incredible. Impossible. He hadn't thought he stood a chance of getting it. But here it was in black and white. He was approved, and for the amount he had applied for.

He stood. Paced the floor. Sat down again to read some more, his mind spinning through a myriad of options. Now he would be able to hire a full crew. Get himself a foreman. More equipment. Bid on more jobs. His lips curled. He had to tell someone. He had to tell her.

He went across to the phone and dialed before he could change his mind about it.

"Mrs. Lewis," he said as soon as the phone was picked up. "Is Lola there?"

Annie beamed. Now this was a good sign. A good sign indeed. He was calling her now. It would only be a matter of time. Just a matter of time.

"Lola's not in, honey. But you can call her on her cell phone. Do you have the number?"

Chaz clenched a fist. No, he didn't have her cell phone number. She hadn't given it to him.

He forced himself to smile. "I'll call her later then. It wasn't really that important."

Annie rang off after telling him what time Lola would probably be back, then dialed Lola's car phone and said with great excitement in her voice, "He called."

Lola, who was battling her way through the noonday traffic on the way to a hairdressing appointment, laughed gleefully into the phone.

"Stage three. Bermuda," she said. Then, "Did he say anything?"

"Just asked where you were."

Lola chortled again. "Did you tell him I was out with another man?"

Annie made a clicking sound with her tongue. "Lola girl, I don't like these games you're playing. One of these days, everything's going to backfire on you. I don't think this man is the kind you can play with. If you want him, you've got to be straight with him."

Lola gave her an, "Um-hmm," and Annie said sharply, "Are you listening to me?"

Lola changed lanes to avoid a speeding 18-wheeler. "Annie, love, you don't understand the men of today. They're different from the ones of your generation. Men these days have to be managed. Trained. Sometimes even leashed. Otherwise, they can do all sorts of damage. You know what I mean?"

Annie didn't know what she meant but, after many years of working closely with Lola, had come to realize that sometimes she just had to leave her be. Lola, as much as she loved her and wanted to save her from pain, would have to learn the really important lessons in life in her own way, in her own time.

"You know the ex-wife is coming to visit?" Annie said now, changing the subject completely.

Lola's heart thudded. "What? What do you mean?"

"I meant to tell you this morning, but you were busy with Camille. The child told me last night. He's very excited about the whole thing. Poor little soul."

Lola chewed on the edge of a nail, her mind working. She probably didn't have anything to worry about on the romantic end with the woman; Chaz surely would not have any interest in her. But what did concern Lola was that she was coming to visit now, after so many years. What was she up to? Would she try to take the boy away from Chaz?

A hard light fired in the backs of Lola's eyes. Well, if that was the case, the woman would soon find out that she had picked the wrong time in Chaz's life to pull a stunt like that. Lola would fight her with everything she had, both barrels loaded. She could be worse than a pit bull when roused.

"Did the child say when?"

Annie shrugged. "Nothing's set, apparently." She adjusted the phone. "Now don't go worrying yourself about it, Lola. I'm sure the woman just wants to see her son. What kind of mother just goes off and leaves her child, after all?"

Lola made a noncommittal sound in the back of her throat. Maybe. . . .

Chapter Twenty-two

Lola dressed with particular care that evening. A dab of perfume behind the left ear, the right, at each temple, a squirt in the air so that the fragrance enveloped her. Black silk stockings with seams up the back. A frilly bustier that enhanced her already-perky bosom. Her hair swept up to sit high on the crown of her head. Deliberate curls cascading over each ear. White diamonds in each lobe and around her neck. A navy floor-length gown of printed Oriental silk. Three-quarter-length gloves. Matching high heels.

She was a vision. She had spent all afternoon at the hairdresser's and then another several hours at the spa, where she had been massaged, plucked, sloughed, and painted. She had finally, after many calls from his office, accepted Senator George Mason's invitation to a particularly high-profile ball in the capital. She had no long-term plans for the senator, of course, but now that Chaz was showing a little bit of interest, she intended to scale back her attentions by just a little. Although she had made him think that he would have access to her every night of the week, she had absolutely no intention of allowing him such freedoms. She was well aware that even though the cow and the milk theory might be a little on the jaded side, there was still some merit to the thinking. And instinct told her that Chaz Kelly would not be an easy bird to catch. He would require a special touch. An expert strategy.

The phone on her bedside table rang, and her skirts made a swishing sound as she moved toward it.

"Yes, hello?"

She smiled at the sound of his voice. Somehow she had known it would be him.

"I called you today, didn't Annie tell you?"

Her lip curled at one corner. Already he was beginning to sound possessive. This was good. This was very good. What would he say when he heard that she was going out, and not with him?

Her voice had a measured calm to it. "She told me. I just haven't had the time to call you back yet. Was it urgent?"

She felt certain that she could hear him grinding his teeth at that.

"What time should I show up tonight? A quarter of eight sound good?"

"Oh," and she took a deliberate pause so that her voice would sound genuinely surprised, regretful, "I forgot to tell you. I have an engagement tonight. It was arranged weeks ago. It completely slipped my mind . . ." She let the remainder of the sentence taper off.

She could hear him breathing on the other end and waited patiently for his response.

After a few moments of silence, he said, "Fine," in a snappy voice and hung up with an abrupt, "Have a good time."

Chaz replaced the phone in its cradle and went to sit before the TV. He flipped on the set and roamed without purpose from one end of the box to the next. He should have known better than to get involved with a woman like her. She was obviously into playing games, blowing hot one moment, cold the next, manipulating her men. Well, he wasn't her man, and she would soon learn that he couldn't be played.

He flipped back to a sports channel and watched the seven o'clock basketball game in moody silence. After just five minutes of staring at the back-and-forth of play, he snapped off the set and stood. Maybe she wasn't playing around with him. He scratched the side of his head. It was possible that she had planned this outing many weeks before. After all, he had only sprung the whole affair business on her just the day before. And she did have a life.

He went to the window and looked out on the curving drive. He was being selfish. Stupid and selfish. She was free to go out with whomever she pleased. That had been part of their agreement. And that was the way he wanted it. No strings. No commitments. No expectations. It was just that the sex had been so good that all day he'd been looking forward to another long and exhausting session with her.

His brow wrinkled. Well, she wouldn't escape him tomorrow. And he would plan things so that she couldn't come up with another reason why she couldn't fulfill her part of the bargain.

Headlights going past on the curving drive drew him to the window again. He caught sight of the tail end of a large luxury-model Mercedes-Benz. His brows snapped together. The senator. Hadn't she told him herself that she intended to marry the man?

"Jamie?" he bellowed as his son's laughter drifted from one of the bedrooms.

When the child answered, Chaz said quickly, "I'm going out for a few minutes. Will you be OK alone? I won't be long."

"I'm all grown-up now, Dad, you don't have to worry about me."

"OK, little man, but you call me on my cell if you need me. All right? I should be no more than fifteen minutes."

"OK, Dad."

Chaz gathered up his keys. He had to see for himself who she was going out with. It didn't matter one way or the other to him, of course, but still, it would be interesting to see what kind of men she liked.

He opened and locked the door behind him, then walked briskly down the cobblestone path that ran between the two houses.

Lola swept down the long staircase in her navy gown. She knew she looked fabulous. Her bosom, her waist, her hips were in just the right proportions. The diamonds in her ears caught the light as she descended with tail of dress in hand.

Annie greeted her at the bottom. "You look wonderful." And she bent closer to whisper, "Is this a good idea, though?"

Lola gave her a squeeze. "It's working. He wasn't very pleased about me going out tonight." She went across to a gilt-framed mirror, checked her hair, and then asked, "where is Senator Mason?"

Chaz stepped back into the shadow of thick shrubbery as the front door opened. His jaw clenched as she stepped out onto the top flagstone. She was a tall woman by anyone's standards, and tonight she appeared almost statuesque. He was stunned by her beauty and poise. His gaze flickered over the man who stood at her side. He was taller than she was. Hell, he was taller than even Chaz was. Secretly Chaz had hoped to find a short pudgy little man with spectacles and a beer belly. But this . . . this senator was in great shape. And he was the kind of man that Chaz knew most women would find to their liking. Damn it. How could he compete with that?

Chaz watched her escort bend toward her ear and gritted his teeth as her laughter rang out. The driver opened the back door for them both, and an unfamiliar hot and cold sensation ran through Chaz as the heavy car door was shut behind them.

Lola forced herself not to look at the bushes to the right of the front stairs. She had only seen him moments before stepping into the car. But, praise be to God, he was there, standing in the shadows, and the expression on his face was very, very stern.

She settled back into the soft leather seat. Tomorrow she would let him have her again. And this time, this time she would pull out all the stops.

Chapter Twenty-three

"Dad, can I go play with Mrs. Lewis today?"

Chaz paused in his busy preparations. "No camp again today? Don't you have any friends there?"

The boy shrugged. "They're boring. Not like the kids in D.C. They never want to do anything fun."

Chaz put a long loaf of crusty French bread into the picnic basket, added crackers, cheese spread, ham.

"What kind of fun things don't they want to do?"

Jamie peered into the basket. "Just things."

"I hope you're not encouraging them to do anything dangerous. No playing with fireworks," he racked his brain, trying to think of the many things children of ten might get into, ". . . or that sort of thing."

Jamie's eyes rounded with innocence. "No, Dad. Of course not."

"Good." Chaz added a bottle of Merlot, two plastic glasses resembling wine flutes.

Jamie stuck a hand into the basket.

"Don't touch that," Chaz admonished. "Your lunch pail is over there."

"But who's it for then?"

Chaz closed the basket. "Your old dad's taking the day off."

"The whole day?"

Chaz nodded. "The whole day."

The little boy grew suddenly excited. "Can I come then? Huh, Dad? Can I?"

Chaz looked down at the child's eager face, and a feeling of shame ran through him. How many times had he told his own flesh and blood that he couldn't take the day off to take him to the movies or the fun park? And now here he was, sneaking off for a day just so he could get himself some more of the great sex he had had before. But wasn't he a man, though? Wasn't he entitled to a life? And he did try his best to give Jamie every comfort. Worry flickered through his eyes. But maybe he needed to give Jamie some other things, too.

He bent to hug his son. "Not this time, sport. But, I promise, tomorrow I'll take you to the water park. Would you like that?"

Jamie nodded. "And can we spend all day?"

Chaz gave him an affectionate tap behind the head.

"Tomorrow we'll spend as long as you like. We'll eat all the hamburgers, hot dogs, cotton candy, and whatever else you like."

"And can I go to Mrs. Lewis today?"

Chaz lifted the basket from the table. "Let's go see."

Lola pulled on a light blue T-shirt, a pair of jeans shorts and white tube socks and topped off the ensemble with matching jean fabric tennis shoes. This entire picnic idea had caught her completely by surprise. The evening before had been a nice one. George Mason had been extremely attentive, barely leaving her side once all evening. She had mingled, posed for photographs, swapped business cards, even gotten involved in a

heated discussion with a congressman from somewhere in Kentucky. But throughout the evening's fes-
tivities she had found herself drifting every so often to
thoughts of Chaz. She found herself wondering about
little things. Had he eaten yet? Was he in bed watching
TV? Had she overplayed her hand? Would he now go
out and find himself another woman? By the end of the
evening, her head had been buzzing with tension, and
when her escort had suggested that they call it a night,
she had agreed, readily. She had not agreed to any future dates but had not closed the door completely on
that possibility. The young senator was a pleasant,
well-mannered man, and maybe had Chaz not been in
the picture . . . But he was in the picture, and for as
long as there was breath in her body, no other woman
would have him.

"Lola honey," Annie's voice drifted up the stairs.
"Chaz is here."

Lola grabbed up a large canvas bag, shoved blanket,
sunglasses, and a few other necessities into its volumi-
nous mouth, and reminded herself to walk, not sprint,
down the staircase.

Chaz looked up at her as soon as she came into
view, his dark eyes sinking into hers.

"Hello there," Lola said, and her heart lifted even
further at the smile on his face.

"I'm leaving this little tyke with Mrs. Lewis," he
said.

Lola exchanged a quick glance with Annie. "Excellent. Excellent. You'll be a good boy, won't you, Jamie?"

The boy nodded. "I'm going to teach Mrs. Lewis
how to play video games."

Annie rolled her eyes. "Oh lord."

Chaz chuckled. "Now take it easy on her, Jamie. OK?"

"OK," the child agreed.

Lola stroked a hand across his head. She was really beginning to like the little thing. He was so lovable when he wasn't tearing up the place. That very thing was still bothering the life out of Annie, too. Why had the boy suddenly become so angelic?

She turned her attention now to Chaz and gave him a buoyant smile.

"Ready to go?"

They walked down the stairs together and out to his truck. He opened the door, handed her in, closed the door behind her. And Lola noted all of this with a pleased nod of her head. So he had not forgotten how to treat a lady.

He opened the driver's side door and climbed in. When he was properly settled, she asked nicely, "Where're we going? Or is it supposed to be a surprise?"

He started the engine. "Assateague State Park. It's not going to be anything ritzy."

Lola gave him a bland look. "Ritzy?"

"Not anything like the event you went to last night." He shifted gears, spun the wheel, headed down the drive.

Lola hid a smile. So she'd been right. He didn't like her going out with other men.

"That was just a charity thing I couldn't get out of."

"And the man you went along with, is he the one you were telling me about? The senator you want to marry?"

Lola shifted her position in the seat so that she could look at him more directly.

"A senator is a good catch, don't you think so?"

He swept through the gates and turned onto the road before saying, "Not that it's any of my business, but if you want your marriage to last, you have to go into it for the right reasons. Take it from someone who knows."

She nodded at him. "That's exactly why I intend to marry for love, and not for any other reason."

Her response appeared to displease him, and they drove for several miles in complete silence. Lola crossed her legs before her, and she noticed with satisfaction that his eyes rested on the curve of a smooth thigh before he shifted them again to the road.

"You know," Lola said, when it became clear that he was not going to say anything else, "you're a very closed person."

He turned to give her a look. "Me? A closed person?"

She gave him a pert, "That's right. You're as tight as a rabbit's behind. If you ask me—"

But whatever else she had intended to say was drowned out by his sudden unexpected guffaw of laughter. He shot her a glance. "OK. OK. Let's start this again."

And, for the next little while, they lapsed into an easy conversation. He told her about his bank loan coming through and about some of the plans he had for expanding his business. Lola listened carefully, making helpful suggestions here and there, but mostly giving him the room to talk. After a while, he asked, "And what about your business concerns? I remember reading somewhere that you're into corporate acquisitions now?"

Lola smiled at him. God, life was great. Here she was, sitting right beside the one man she had ever really wanted, talking about business and other things that really mattered.

"I started out in construction, you know."

Chaz nodded. "I know. They used to call you the female Donald Trump."

Lola laughed. "Well, that's one of the nicer things they've called me. It was hard for a woman in that kind of industry. I had to prove myself. Show that I could be just as tough as, if not tougher than, the boys."

"And you did."

She cranked down the window and let the wind pour into the truck.

"I did some things in those early days that I'm not proud of." She examined her thumbnail. She had never said this to anyone at all before, and Chaz, who had been observing her out of the corners of his eyes, reached across to cover her hand with one of his.

"What's done is done. I wouldn't worry too much about it now."

"Uhm," Lola agreed. "I buy and sell companies now. That's where the big money is these days. The trick is to buy a big ungainly company, break it up into smaller parts, and then sell those parts off to other takers."

"So that's all you do now? No more tearing down old buildings and putting up hotels, condos, that sort of thing?"

She looked down at the hand that still covered hers. The simple act of compassion, of caring, had almost brought a flood of tears to her eyes. It had been a hard struggle in those early years when she was building her business. She had worked day and night making deals, calling in favors, using muscle when she had to. But she had been tireless, driven, and the only thing that had really thrown her was news of his marriage. She had managed to convince herself that he would marry no one but her. But he had married, and she had told herself that she didn't care. She had deliberately let herself grow harder, colder, more ruthless. The pursuit of money had become the only thing of real importance in her life. That and Annie.

"Yes," she said simply, "that's all I do now." And she looked at him with eyes that were damp around the edges.

The simplicity of her answer and the hidden hurt in her eyes stirred something deep in Chaz. Something he had thought was long dead. And, before he could change his mind about it, he leaned over and kissed her flush on the mouth. Her lips responded immediately to his, and the unexpected sweetness of it caused Chaz to draw back quickly. What was he doing? He had promised himself that he would never kiss her. If he wasn't careful, he was going to lose himself in this woman, and then she would go off and very calmly marry some other man.

He shifted gears, cast another sidelong look at her. She was such an interesting blend of vulnerability and rock-hard strength. In many ways, the perfect woman. For him anyway. A frown huddled between his brows at the thought. It was clear he was losing his mind, and all because of a little sex.

He cleared his throat. "I thought it'd be fun to do some kite flying before we eat. Are you up for it?"

Lola, who had been sitting completely still for the last several minutes, afraid of moving, afraid of breaking the unexpected rapport that had suddenly sprung up between them, almost jumped at the sound of his voice.

"Kites?" she said. It had been years since she had indulged in anything so absolutely frivolous. A feeling of deep happiness swept her up. "I'm up for anything. Within reason, of course." And, her eyes sparkled up at him.

Chaz returned her smile. "Good. There's a little place pretty close to the entrance to the park where we can stop and pick one out. They've a great selection there."

They drove on in companionable silence, and Lola lay back against the headrest and prayed that whatever it was that was happening between them would continue.

Chapter Twenty-four

The rest of the day passed all too quickly. First they stopped for the kites and Lola spent a glorious half an hour browsing through a very wide selection of box kites, bird kites, buzz kites. Kites with single strings and those with double. She finally settled on a very colorful red, blue, and gold kite with an aggressive-looking snarl painted across its face. She held the kite up with a triumphant, "This one, I think."

Chaz walked across to examine her choice and, after turning the kite over and back a couple of times, said, "You like this one, huh?"

"I can always pick a winner," Lola told him, her eyes flashing flirtatiously at him.

He chuckled. "We'll see."

Chaz shelled out the cash, gathered up the kite, and then took her by the hand. They walked down the little collection of outdoor stands, stopping every so often to examine the offerings of each vendor. There were interesting little trinkets, large copper pots twisted into intricate designs, handmade soaps, framed pictures made from pressed petals. And, every so often, Chaz would pick up an item and inquire, "Do you like this?"

They walked all the way down to the very last vendor, discussing the relative merits of each, joking back

and forth at some of the more outrageous items. And
Lola, in a moment of impulsive exuberance, reached
up and planted a warm kiss on the side of his face.
They exchanged a look, and Chaz said a little gruffly,
"What was that for?"

But Lola saw through the gruffness and understood
instinctively that her little gesture of affection had
pleased him.

They went for ice cream next, and for the first time
in a long while Lola indulged in a large chocolate-
dipped waffle cone, with a double scoop of butter
pecan and mint chocolate chip. She ate the entire thing
with great enjoyment, licking the dribbles of cream
from the sides and backs of her hand and exclaiming in
a voice that made Chaz laugh, "God! I think I've died
and gone to heaven!"

He rubbed a stroke of cream from the corner of her
mouth with the flat of a thumb and said in a bemused
manner, "You're one of the most puzzling women I've
ever met."

And, with that comment ringing in her ears, they
walked back to the truck and got in. The hours that followed were spent running up and down a wide-open
expanse in the park, with the kite trailing drunkenly behind. Lola threw herself wholeheartedly into the en-
deavor, shrieking with laughter as the kite stubbornly
refused to rise. And Chaz, much to Lola's delight,
charged back and forth across the grass, bellowing instructions and occasionally tripping over clumps of un-
even turf. After much fruitless effort, he finally
collapsed on his back beneath the confines of a wide-
branched maple tree and declared in a voice that sent

Lola into additional convulsions, "What do you say we turn the damn thing into firewood?"

Lola fanned him with a hand and then reached into the hamper for a bottle of water. She cracked the cap off with a twist of her wrist, took a tiny swallow, and then handed the rest to him.

"Have some. It'll make you feel so much better."

She lay back beside him, resting her head on the curve of an arm. It was a glorious day. Hot bright blue sky. Beautiful little breeze. White clouds, too fat and lazy to move. She sucked in a delicious breath. Now this was what life was really all about. The simple things. She sighed in a luxurious manner. Even though by anyone's standards she was a very rich woman, the money had never been able to give her this feeling of total and utter peace.

Chaz turned onto his side and leaned over her so that his head blotted out the sun.

"You having a good time?"

Lola lifted a hand to his cheek. His skin was hot and smooth and she ran the tips of her fingers beneath the curve of each eye, across a thick eyebrow, down the straight bridge of his nose.

"I've never had a better time."

He lowered his head and took her lips in a quick kiss. Lola held the back of his neck lightly and did not resist him when he pulled away much too soon. His eyes burned into hers.

"How much of a risk taker are you?"

Lola lifted a leg and gently massaged the curve of his crotch with her knee.

"I'm sure I can keep up with anything you might have in mind."

He lowered his head again and bit the blunt of her chin.

"Really?"

"Yes. Really."

His tongue traced the inner curve of her lower lip and Lola opened her mouth to give him deeper access. Her hand drifted down to his zipper, and she yanked it down and stuck her hand inside.

Chaz groaned in a low undertone as her fingers found their target.

"Can we do this? We're not kids, you know."

"Uhmm," Lola agreed against his mouth. "Exactly right."

Her fingers closed over the hot pulsating length of him, and she moved her hand slowly in the rhythm she knew he liked, watching his eyes for signs of pleasure, increasing her movements as the muscles in his neck bunched and released. Bunched and released.

Chaz allowed her to have her way with him until finally he could stand no more of it. He cast a quick look around the secluded little spot and then pulled her to her feet. His hands made quick work of her pants, pushing them down so that they languished somewhere between ankle and mid-thigh. He spun her expertly so that the side of her face rested against the smooth tree trunk and in a hoarse voice asked, "Are you comfortable?"

Her half-impatient, "Come on," caused him to bend his head into the curve of her neck, pull the slip of black bikini underwear down to join her pants, and then in one solid thrust enter her from behind.

Lola shuddered as he dragged her backward, positioning her even higher against his thighs. Her nails curled against the bark of the tree and spasmodic gasps of breath escaped her as he began to move. She pressed herself back against him and he groaned her name in reply. Lola closed her eyes and held on to the tree trunk. Jesus, she had never done anything this wild, this absolutely crazy. But this man, this handsome, sexy man, brought out the animal in her. She gasped his name and thrust herself at him, giving all of herself, not caring that they were out in the open. Not caring about anything at all.

The pleasure rose higher and higher until Lola knew that she couldn't hold on any longer.

She turned to look at him with fierce eyes, commanding him, begging him. His hands tangled in her hair, and he dragged her head back against his shoulder.

"Tell me that your senator can make you feel this way."

And he lifted her off the ground, balancing her on his thighs and yet somehow still managing to maintain the pulsing, throbbing rhythm.

Lola sobbed and thrashed wildly.

"Tell me," he said again.

"He . . . he can't."

And with those words he gave her the release she was seeking. His legs shook, her muscles trembled, and then in one final shuddering wave, the climax took them.

Chaz eased her back down onto the blanket spread

at the bottom of the tree trunk, and Lola, with salty tears running from each eye, said, "One of these days . . ."

He tidied her with a hand, pulling up her zipper, snapping the button back into place, wiping the streaky tears from her face with the tips of his fingers. When he was through he asked, "What's going to happen one of these days?"

She turned toward him, and he held her.

"Does nothing ever touch you so deeply that . . . well, that you lose complete control of . . . of everything?"

He slipped a hand beneath her shirt and stroked the smooth run of her spine.

"No. I never lose control. But then again, you have to remember that men tend not to be as emotional about things as women."

"What about when you fall in love with someone?"

His hand paused and then resumed its progress along the flat of her back.

"I don't think I've ever been in love like that. There was a time in high school, though," and he laughed in a regretful manner. "A time when I thought I'd found the girl. But what do kids really know about that sort of thing? It's all lust and passion at that age. Although, for me, with her, it was different."

Lola had gone ice-cold as he continued to speak. She knew exactly which girl he was referring to. Even though it was so many years ago, she hadn't forgotten the name. Veronica Simms. The sports agent's daughter. The leader of the cheerleading squad. They had been such a ridiculous cliché. The captain of the football team and the head cheerleader. They had dated each other all throughout their senior year, and she, little Sadie Green, had been shunted to the side and forgotten.

Even though it irked her to know, she found that she had to ask it.

"So, what ever happened to this girl? The one you cared so deeply about? Did you just drift apart?"

He went quiet for such a long while that Lola wondered if somehow he had fallen asleep. But just as she was about to ask him that very thing, he said in a blank voice, "Kids are stupid, you know. And God knows they can be cruel. But there is no excuse for," he sighed, "for what I let happen."

Lola propped herself up on an elbow. This was a story she hadn't heard.

"What happened?"

He shifted her closer. "God, it's been a long time since I've thought about this. I can't help wondering where she is now. She's probably got a husband and five bawling kids by now, but it would be nice to just see her again. For years I've wanted to tell her how sorry I was for what I did . . . for the fact that we drifted apart. But too many years have gone by. It wouldn't matter to her now. It was just a high school thing. . . ."

Lola sat up. So, he had been in love with two different girls in high school. She didn't want to hear any more. Why it was that she hadn't just completely given up on him was something she would never know. How wrong she had been to think that in high school he had considered her to be his friend. Hell, he didn't even remember her. And all he could do was rattle on about his ridiculous infatuation with this other woman.

"I'm getting hungry," she said abruptly, and proceeded to root around in the picnic hamper.

Chaz sat up, too, and he watched her frenetic searching without comment. Something had obviously upset her, but what that something was he had no idea. Sometimes women could be such perplexing and moody creatures. He had almost given up trying to understand them.

"I hope you like what I packed. I wasn't sure what you'd like, so I threw in a little of everything. Some ham, bread, cheese, pâté, wine."

Lola pulled out the loaf of twisty French bread. She was already over her momentary fit of pique. It was ridiculous to brood over the fact that he didn't remember a chubby little high school girl called Sadie Green. She didn't exist any longer anyway. So what did it matter?

She sliced the bread in half and then again down the middle.

"What do you want? Ham and cheese or just . . ." Her voice tapered off. "What's the matter?"

He lifted a hand and traced the soft raised skin behind her left ear. "You've a large scar there. I'd never noticed it before."

Lola gave him a matter-of-fact little look. "The leavings of reconstructive surgery."

His eyebrows lifted. "You? Cosmetic surgery?"

Lola loaded one-half of the bread with ham, cheese, mustard. She handed him the sandwich and then set to work on the other half.

"It wasn't cosmetic surgery done for frivolous reasons, believe me. It was . . . well, let's just say that my face was pretty badly . . . damaged."

Chaz lifted a finger to stroke the welt of skin behind her ear and a hair-fine shiver went through her.

"An accident?"

She finished making her sandwich, took a bite of it, and then said in a very conversational manner, "No, it was deliberate. Very deliberate."

His eyebrows snapped together. "What do you mean . . . deliberate? Do you mean someone did this to you?"

Lola took another bite of sandwich. This was not something that she enjoyed talking about; it brought back too many memories of things that were better off forgotten. But since he had asked with such concern in his voice. . .

"It happened during one of my first big construction jobs. My competition didn't think I had won the contract fairly. So . . ."

Chaz had put his sandwich down and was staring at her now with a mixture of compassion, incredulity, and anger.

"So what happened to the bastard who did this to you?"

Lola smiled, and her eyes glinted like the edge of a steel blade. "Oh, him? He's no longer with us."

Chaz shook his head. "Jesus. I'll have to remember never to cross you, lady."

She patted his hand as if to reassure him. "That was a long time ago. I'm a totally different person today. And just so you don't get the wrong impression, I didn't have anything to do with his demise. Not anything direct, anyway."

Chaz flopped over onto his back. He was beginning to get the feeling that this woman sitting beside him was as strong as any man; she certainly commanded more power than most. And he wasn't at all certain that she could be beaten in any kind of fight, fair or not.

Lola chewed on the sandwich and cast a little surreptitious glance at him. She had obviously shocked him with her disclosure. But what could she do? Lie to him? If he was going to love her, he would have to love all of her, warts and all. And lord, did she have some warts.

She reached into the hamper for the wine, examined the label, and then poured some of the sparkling liquid into one of the plastic wineglasses. She offered it to him with, "What're you thinking?"

Chaz accepted the offering of wine, took a measured sip of it, and then pointed at a white cumulus cloud.

"Would you say that was a . . . dog? Or a house?"

Lola gave him a startled look. *A dog or a house?* She reached down and with thumb and forefinger spread apart the lower and upper lids of his left eyeball.

"Are you on something?"

He batted her hand away with a laughing, "Did you never do this as a child? Come on. It's fun."

Lola cocked her head and stared up at the sky. She couldn't see a single thing. Not a dog, house, or cow, for that matter.

Chaz looped a long arm about her waist. "You've got to look at the sky lying on the flat of your back. Come on. Give it a try."

Lola obliged him by lying back on the blanket. She popped her sunglasses onto her nose and squinted up at the blue. She was no good at all at these imaginative things.

Chaz pulled her closer. "OK. First thing is you've got to relax. So breathe. In, and then out. That's right," he encouraged. "In, and then out."

Lola chuckled. "I still don't see a single thing. They're all just clouds to me."

He pointed again. "OK. Take a look at that one. What do you think?"

Lola considered the large white mass for a second. "Ah . . . a balance sheet?"

Chaz poked her in the ribs. "Wrong. Try again."

"OK. A . . . fat CEO with a large bald head and jowls."

Chaz laughed. "You're hopeless."

"Thank you," she said chirpily, and she snuggled her head against the rise of his chest.

They lay together in this manner for countless minutes, until the rise and fall, rise and fall of his chest slowly, gradually, lulled Lola into full-blown sleep.

Chaz watched her as she slept, his eyes flickering over the pert little nose, high cheekbones, generous mouth now parted with just a snatch of white visible. She was an amazing woman. A simply amazing woman.

He sighed in one long and expansive breath. Which man in his right mind, after he had had a taste of her, would have the strength to turn her away?

Chapter Twenty-five

Lola returned home in a buoyant mood. It had been a wonderful day and she couldn't have asked for a more idyllic one had she sat and planned it herself. She stood at the front door watching Chaz until she could no longer see him on the cobblestone path; then she shut and locked the door and went up to her bedroom suite. Already the hunger for him was rising in her, but she wouldn't give in to the feelings. She would take a long cold shower and then go right off to bed. She was too full with the remains of the day to eat anything at all. Besides, Annie had probably had a long and tiring day with the boy and was well deserving of an early night.

Lola opened the door to the suite. The bedroom was immaculate as always, the Tiffany bedside table lamp had been left on, and a cool waft of air puffed from one of the inset air conditioners.

Lola went across to the answering machine, pressed the button. Three messages. She sat on the edge of the bed and began to listen to them. The first two were from Senator Mason. He was inviting her to accompany him to Paris and then on to Rome. He had called back the second time to leave the number of his New York condo.

She reached for the tiny white pad that always sat

right next to the phone. She didn't intend to go to Paris with George Mason, of course, but she would have to call him to explain why she couldn't go with him.

She was just getting herself a pen when the phone on the little table began to ring. She let it buzz a couple of times before lifting the receiver to say, "Lola here. . . . Chaz." The surprise in her voice was genuine. She hadn't thought that she'd hear from him again before at least the morning.

"Listen," he said. "I've been promising Jamie that I'd take him to one of these amusement parks . . . so we're going to do that tomorrow. I know it's not really the kind of thing that you corporate women usually enjoy, but would you like to come along? I think the boy would enjoy it."

Lola grinned at the phone. "Believe me, we corporate types have a lot more fun than you might think."

She heard his husky laugh and knew exactly what thoughts her words had brought to mind.

"So what do you think?"

"Just try and keep me away."

She hung up the phone with smiling eyes. He was beginning to like her. It was as plain and clear as the nose on her face.

She took a couple of spins about the bedroom with arms wrapped tightly about herself. Everything was going to be just fine; she could just feel it.

The next morning, Lola was up bright and early. She dressed in a conservative black one-piece swimsuit with simple white piping around the edges. She called Chaz at just before eight to inquire, "When're we leaving?"

His reply sent her hustling downstairs for coffee and a bite to eat. She swept into the kitchen, pressed a kiss to the side of Annie's face, and then proceeded to rummage about in one of the cupboards for coffee. She pushed tins this way and that, making a general racket as she hunted for the characteristic brown sack of dark-roasted Blue Mountain coffee.

Annie came over when the noise was finally a little too much for her.

"What're you doing to my cupboards?"

Lola paused in her hunting for just a minute. "The Blue Mountain coffee. Where is it?"

Annie pushed her aside. "Come, honey. Come. Let me find it. Why didn't you just ask me for it instead of turning the entire place upside down? Just sit there for a bit," and she proceeded to mutter to herself about young people drinking altogether too much coffee.

Lola perched herself on a stool and paid absolutely no attention to Annie's good-natured grumblings.

"Annie love," she said after a moment's thought. "How would you like to go to the villa in Bermuda?"

Annie turned with the sack of coffee in hand. "Bermuda?"

Lola gave her a pleased as punch look. "We haven't gone all year."

Annie poured dark crystals of coffee into the percolator, flipped the switch on.

"You're going to go off on vacation now? Just when things are improving with Chaz?"

"But that's the thing." Lola beamed. "I'm going to ask him to come, too. It would be nice to just laze around on the sand, wouldn't it? Right there on the ocean. No one around for miles but us?"

Annie went back to check on the golden hunks of French toast. She turned one square over, added a bit more egg batter to the exposed top.

"Lola, you have to begin spending more time with the little boy. That man will never marry you unless he figures you'll make a good mother for his son. No matter how good and perfect everything else is between you. Are you listening to me?"

"I'm listening," Lola said. "That's why I'm spending the entire day at the water park today. What do you think of the suit?" She stood and raised her T-shirt.

Annie nodded. "Good choice. I like it. Now sit and eat."

Her face settled into lines of disapproval as Lola drew breath to tell her that she really didn't care for anything too heavy.

"Maybe one piece of French toast, some juice, and coffee?"

Annie placed two slabs of golden toast on a plate along with a short link of sausage.

"How're you going to be running about a park all day, chasing after a ten-year-old-boy, on an empty stomach?"

She put the plate down before Lola and ordered, "And eat every last thing. You're beginning to lose weight, and the good Lord knows that you're skin and bones as it is."

Lola swallowed a chuckle. If she was skin and

bones, she certainly didn't want to see the woman who was considered to have a little bit of flesh on her body.

"OK, Annie love, but just to please you. I don't know what it is, but of late I just don't feel hungry at all."

Annie gave her a sharp look. "Have you been getting sick in the mornings?"

Lola laughed. "Don't worry, I'm not pregnant."

Annie brought over the steaming cup of coffee, added two lumps of sugar, a touch of milk. Getting pregnant outside the sanctity of marriage was no laughing matter as far as she was concerned. And Lola's dear sainted mother would turn in her grave if such a disgrace fell on her daughter.

Lola squeezed a dollop of maple syrup onto the slab of toast, folded the bread in half, and then took a crunchy bite. She chewed with obvious enjoyment, wiped a sticky smudge from one corner of her mouth.

"So how did things go yesterday with the child? Did he blow up anything?"

Annie fixed herself a plate and then came over to sit opposite Lola.

"He was as good as you could want him to be." She took a sip from her glass of juice. "I also promised him that if he wasn't, I would wallop his backside but good."

"So you don't think he's planning to do anything spectacular?"

Annie took a moment to consider this.

"I think what that child needs more than anything else is a mother. You know, the kind who will kiss his boo-boos, tuck him into bed at night, read him bedtime stories. That sort of thing." She shook her head. "That mother of his deserves to be horsewhipped. Imagine just getting up and leaving your child like that. And then not even coming for a visit every now and again?"

"Uhmm," Lola agreed. "Poor little thing. Maybe all he needed was a nice stable environment with women around. He's definitely taken to you, though, Annie."

"And he will take to you, too, if you make him feel important. Figuring out most kids isn't a difficult thing to do. All they need is a little bit of love, a little bit of attention. And, believe me, sometimes for the good of them, you just have to whip their little butts."

Lola nodded. "Well, at least the mother looks like she's going to start spending some time with him."

Annie sliced a bit of sausage, put it in her mouth. "I just hope she's not doing it to mess with Chaz."

Lola's eyes hardened. "Well, Chaz isn't all alone now. So if she wants to get to him, she's going to have to come through me. And you know I don't—"

But the ringing of the doorbell interrupted her. "It's them," she said, and she wiped both corners of her mouth, flung the napkin on the countertop.

"Will you be all right here all alone?" she asked, anxious for a minute and nibbling at the corner of a nail.

Annie shooed her from the kitchen. "I'm perfectly well and healthy, so why shouldn't I be all right?"

Lola picked up her shoulder bag, which she had placed near the front door.

"I'll have my cell phone with me. So any problems at all, call me right away. OK?"

"Go on and have fun," Annie said. And she stood at the door waving as Lola climbed into the front seat of Chaz's truck.

Lola buckled herself in and then turned to Jamie with, "All set to have some fun today?"

The boy looked at her in a bland manner. "Is Mrs. Lewis coming?"

Lola exchanged a look with Chaz. "Not today. But I promise you we're going to have a great time. Look," and she removed a little package from her bag. "I brought hats for everyone." She put a cap on her head and pulled at the visor. "Pretty cool, huh?"

"Dad," Jamie said, and he totally ignored the hats in Lola's hand. "Can Mrs. Lewis come?"

Chaz started the truck. "No, Jamie. Mrs. Lewis is going to take a well-deserved rest today. You can't have her all to yourself every day, you know. She needs some time to herself."

The boy's face crumpled by just a bit. "But she likes playing with me. And she'll be lonely if I'm not there."

Chaz shifted gears and consoled him with, "You'll see her when we get back. Maybe you can bring her back a nice little gift. Hmm?"

Lola's eyebrows lifted. Poor little spud. Annie had been exactly right. The boy needed his mother, and he had bonded with Annie because . . . She pulled her visor down against the sun and slitted her eyes in thought. Because . . . Annie was warm and motherly, and even when she was angry about something, it was still understood that she loved you anyway.

She shifted in her seat. Well, Lola would just have to convince the child that she loved him, too. It had been a mistake not spending time with him.

"How about we play a game?" she said as soon as they had merged with the highway traffic.

Chaz seized the idea immediately, glancing in the rearview mirror at the slightly glum face of his son. Lola gave Chaz a conspiratorial wink.

"OK. The first one to spot a car with Washington, D.C., plates gets—"

"—A hot dog," Chaz piped in.

The boy caught his father's eye in the rearview mirror. "How about a hot dog and a hamburger?"

"Perfect," Lola agreed. "A hot dog and a hamburger."

Jamie looked at her with renewed interest. "Does it have to be a car? Or can it be a truck, or a . . . motorcycle?"

Lola looked at Chaz. "What do you think, Dad? Can we include bikes and trucks and birds and planes?"

The little boy chuckled. "Birds and planes are out."

Chaz agreed with a solemn nod. "I'm afraid I'm going to have to rule against birds and planes. I'm with you, Jamie boy. Those are definitely out."

And for the next little while Lola threw herself into the game, deliberately pointing out vehicles that were completely outside the rules of the game. By the time they were almost at the water park, Jamie was laughing outright and cheating just as heartily as she was herself.

Chaz threw her several admiring glances, and after he had parked the truck and taken note of its exact location in the sprawling parking lot, he came around to link arms with her on one side and Jamie on the other.

Lola grinned at Chaz, and rubbed a hand across the top of Jamie's head.

"Last one in loses his hamburger," and she took off running, with the child shrieking with laughter just behind.

The rest of the day passed in a similar manner. Jamie, who had been planning the water park trip for months, knew exactly where it was that he wanted to go. First they hit the waterslides and then the raging rapids. The boy laughed heartily when his father and Lola were both thoroughly doused with water on the white river rafting ride. And Jamie dragged at Lola's hand and begged so nicely that she be allowed to accompany him on one of the most fear-inspiring roller coasters in the park that Lola hadn't the heart to resist him. After the stomach-twisting, heart-stopping ride, she said to Chaz, who had wisely stayed on the ground, "I am truly never, ever going to do that again . . . *in my entire life.*"

Both father and son laughed heartily at that, and a warm feeling crept in to nestle somewhere deep within Lola's bosom. This was what she had yearned for all these many years. A family. A good man to call her very own. And now, miraculously, she had found what she had been searching for.

They spent the entire day at the park, snacking on cinnamon-dipped churros, ice-cream sticks, hot dogs, and Jamie's favorite: onion-smothered cheeseburgers.

And, finally, with the air turning a little cool around them, Chaz coaxed Jamie away from yet another plunge from a rope overhanging one of the pools designed for that very purpose.

"Time to go, little man."

Jamie turned beseeching eyes in her direction, and Lola laughed and said, "Chaz, I think your son sees me as a soft touch. Tell you what," she said to the child. "Let's go look for a present for Mrs. Lewis. OK?"

They browsed through a long string of shops, hunting through bins stocked with stuffed animals, pens, mugs, T-shirts. Finally, the boy held up a finely wrought silver and gold chain with a locket hanging from one end of it. Lola showed him how to snap the locket open and explained that miniature pictures of loved ones were put there.

"Maybe Mrs. Lewis can put a picture of me there then, huh?" the child asked, his eyes bright and enthusiastic about the idea. "Just so she doesn't forget me?"

Lola stroked the back of his neck. "Are you going somewhere sometime soon?" And she looked at Chaz for confirmation of this.

"Well, Dad said that we can't live with you for always. And Mrs. Lewis lives with you."

Lola bent and impulsively kissed the little cheek. "Don't worry too much about that now," she said. "Wherever you are, Mrs. Lewis will be able to come and visit."

And with that, they all piled back into the truck and Lola, who was genuinely exhausted by then, pulled on her final reserves of strength to entertain the child with a singalong, all the way back home.

Chapter Twenty-six

It was close to midnight and Lola had just settled in for a long night of well-earned sleep when the phone on the bedside table rang. She opened an eye, glanced at the face of her watch, and smiled. Booty call. It had to be. No one else would even think to call her at such an hour.

"Chaz," she said, practically purring his name into the phone.

"Jamie's sick," he said without preamble. "Can you come? He's asking for Mrs. Lewis, but I don't want to get her up out of bed."

Lola sat up, the playfulness with which she had answered the phone gone.

"I'll come. What's the matter with him? Have you called for an ambulance?"

She was already halfway into her clothes, hopping on one leg as she got into her sweats.

"He's got a case of pretty bad stomach cramps, with diarrhea. And, he's crying and can't sleep. I don't know. . . ." He paused, cleared his throat. "I think it may have something to do with his mother." He sighed. "I'll tell you when you get here."

Lola put the phone down, grabbed a light jacket, and sprinted down the front stairs, taking two of them at a time. And all the way down, her mind was working. Doctors didn't make house calls anymore these days, but there were several who would if she asked them to.

She was through the front door and down the cobblestone path in record time, her heart beating like a triphammer in her chest. Poor little kid. What a thing to happen, and just after he had had such a good time at the water park, too. And what had Chaz meant when he'd said he thought it might have something to do with the mother?

She jabbed the front doorbell with a finger and waited anxiously. She felt just like a mother with a sick child. She looked at the face of her watch and then jabbed the doorbell again. Where in the world was Chaz?

She was just about to hit the bell again when the door was opened and Chaz stood there with an unusually calm expression on his face. She brushed by him with an abrupt, "Where is he? In his bedroom? Which one?"

The questions followed one another in rapid succession, and Chaz was only able to get out, "Bedroom. Yes. Down the hall," before she had disappeared toward the back of the house.

He followed and came to stand behind her as Lola positioned herself gently on the lip of the bed. She rested her hand on the side of the child's face and released a pent-up breath. Good. No fever.

"Where does it hurt, sweetie?"

Jamie pointed to his stomach and turned eyes that still held the residual traces of tears in her direction.

"Is Mrs. Lewis coming?" he asked in a tight little voice that almost broke Lola's heart.

"Do you think you really need Mrs. Lewis, or can we let her sleep?"

He pondered this for a moment. "I think I can make it without her," he said. "Does she need a lot of sleep?"

Lola smiled. "Just the ordinary amount. But I think she just went off to bed, so . . . ," and she reached forward to gently stroke his stomach, "can you put up with me and your dad for just a little while?"

The child nodded. "OK."

"Good," Lola agreed. "Tell you what, though. Would you like to hear a story?" And she brought both of her legs up to lie on the flat of the bed.

"Stories are boring."

Lola tucked the blanket up around the boy. "Not this one. This story is a very different one. It has action. Adventure. Money. Power. It's all about how this lonely chubby little girl became a millionaire."

She caught his interest with that, and after a moment of thinking about it, he said, "Oh, you mean she became a rapper like Fifty Cent?"

Lola chuckled. "No. She didn't become a rapper. She went into building hotels because she figured out that that was where the big money was."

She rubbed the flat of her palm in a slow circle across his stomach. "How're you feeling now?" She'd already decided that she would call on the services of one of her doctor friends should Jamie's symptoms grow any worse during the night.

"I feel all right."

Chaz, who had been standing silently behind her, said now, "Would you like that cup of hot chocolate now, son? It might make you feel a lot better."

Lola nodded at the child. "Have a little bit, it'll help your tummy."

Chaz smiled at her. "Don't start that story until I get back. I want to hear about that little girl, too."

He was gone and back in only minutes, balancing a thick ceramic cup in one hand and an anti-diarrheal medicine in the other.

Chaz came to sit on the bed, too, and Lola took the cup.

"When did he have the last dose?"

Chaz checked his watch. "About four hours ago."

"OK, big boy," Lola said. "Just half a tablet for you this time." She gave the child a sip of the hot liquid and then the tablet that she had broken neatly in two.

Jamie took everything with no complaint, and after he had swallowed half the cup of hot chocolate, she settled down to the telling of the story with the child on one side of her and Chaz on the other.

She began the tale as any good storyteller of fables would, with, "Once upon a time." But the story she told was no fable—it was the story of her life thus far.

She was careful to leave out the parts that Chaz would recognize. So she picked up the story after high school, and very soon she was deep within the pockets of her memories, telling the exciting parts, skipping over the parts that still brought an ice-cold feeling to her soul. She told of how the little girl had evolved from ugly duckling to beautiful swan. And, as with any good spinner of yarns, her voice rose and fell dramatically with the telling of the tale.

Halfway into the thick of the story, she looked down and saw that the child had gone off to sleep. Lola shifted carefully so as not to wake the boy, and Chaz followed suit. They both crept from the room, turning out the light as the door was quietly closed behind them.

Lola followed Chaz into his bedroom. "Do you think it was something he ate at the park?"

He closed the bedroom door and pulled her into his arms.

"Thank you," he said simply, and he lowered his head to take her lips in a very tender kiss.

Lola's startled breath mingled with his, and she kissed him back softly, holding his face between her hands. When he lifted his head, her eyes were bright with sudden understanding. Annie had been right. Finding love, growing love, keeping love had nothing to do with strategy or game playing. It had to do with this. This sharing. This caring. This very deep feeling of . . . commitment?

She bent her head against the flat of his chest. Oh lord. Now she'd really done it. She'd only meant to love him just a little. Not like this. She had wanted *him* to be the one who was madly, passionately in love with *her*.

God. Why had it happened this way? It wasn't right. It wasn't fair. She didn't have him totally wrapped around her finger. She blinked rapidly at him, her eyes containing traces of worry. In fact, he seemed to have her wrapped very securely about his.

Chaz lifted her chin with a finger. "What's wrong?"

She pulled out of his arms and turned blindly away, her eyes hunting for something, anything, to distract him. Her gaze settled on the bookcase close to his bed.

"Oh," she said in a croaky voice, "your high school yearbook."

She went across to pull it from the shelf and sat on the foot of the bed. Chaz, sensing that there was something amiss but having no clue as to what it was, came across to sit beside her. She appeared uncharacteristically jumpy, and he rubbed a hand up and down her back, hoping that might soothe her.

Lola flipped open the yearbook. She hadn't seen this one in ages. Senior year 1986. She had gotten rid of her copy right after graduation and had sworn then that she would never look at these photographs again.

But here she was, looking "never" right squarely in the face.

She turned rapidly past the pages that held pictures of her, but Chaz stuck his finger out to stop the flow of pages.

"Sadie . . . ," he muttered.

Lola bit the tip of her tongue. "What?" she said, her head flashing about to look at him. Had he just called her Sadie? Had he known who she was all along? Had he just been playing with her?

"Remember in the park the other day, I was telling you about a little girl from high school? The one I . . . liked."

"Right," Lola said, nodding. Yes. Of course she remembered *that*. He had spent a ridiculous amount of time talking about some woman or the other. Did he think that she had gone suddenly soft in the head? How could she possibly forget a thing like that?

Chaz tapped the smooth white page with a finger. "That's her."

Lola looked with blind eyes. "What's her?"

Chaz shifted the book onto his lap. "Her name was . . . is . . . I think she's still alive. Sadie. Sadie Green."

Lola swallowed. Coughed. Swallowed again.

Chaz gave her a look of great concern. "Are you coming down with something now, too? Maybe it's a virus." He got to his feet. "You'd better take some stomach medicine now before it hits."

Lola laughed. Stomach medicine? At a time like this? Was he out of his mind? Didn't he understand what he'd just done? He remembered her. And not only that, he remembered her with fondness. With affection. She stood and then immediately sat again.

"All right," Chaz said. "It's coming. You can't make it to the bathroom, right?" And he nodded as though he had come to a sudden decision. "I'll carry you."

"No," Lola said, waving him away. "I'm fine. Perfectly fine. I'm not sick at all. I promise you."

She tried her best to hold on to the sudden feeling of exuberance. Should she tell him? Could she tell him? How would he take it? She sucked in a breath. Why hadn't she listened to Annie and told him earlier on? Her reasons for not doing so had been irrational, twisted. She fully admitted that now. She had wanted him to fall hard for her, and then, then she would have revealed what her name used to be. Sadie Green. Sadie Green from high school. The poor chubby little girl whom he had just tossed away. What an asinine motivation. What an absolutely ridiculous thing to have done. But what could she do now?

She covered her mouth with a hand. God, she was in such a mess.

"Are you sure you're feeling OK?"

He still looked at her with very concerned eyes, and Lola experienced a wave of unrelenting guilt. She had to do something to make up for this. Maybe then, when she told him, he might forgive her.

She swallowed the dryness away from her throat. "What were you saying on the phone about Jamie's mother being part of the reason why he's sick?"

Chaz sighed. Sat on the bed again. "I've never told anyone this. . . ." He gave a cracked laugh. "I don't even know why I'm telling you. It's something I'm not proud of. But," and he shrugged, "I got married . . ."

"Yes," Lola prodded. She knew that. In fact, she was quite sure that she knew most things about him. But, of course, he wasn't to know that.

"Well, I knew that she . . . the woman I married didn't really love me for me. She loved the lifestyle." He paused to give Lola a look that almost challenged her to disbelieve him. "I used to play for the NFL. You probably wouldn't know that unless you were a fan of the game. It was a long time ago now. Anyway," and he seemed to grow impatient with the telling of the story, "I married this woman . . . Veronica Simms . . . not really for the right reasons, either. I was young; she was beautiful. We went to some great parties. Had a really good time with each other. I did some of the things that all professional athletes do when the money is there, the perks are there, the groupies. You know. All of that. Anyway, soon into it, I messed up my knee pretty badly and suddenly everything I'd worked so hard for up until then was gone. The lifestyle. The celebrity.

The parties. Who wants a washed-up football player around?"

Lola came across to sit beside him, and she draped an arm about him. The pain in his eyes tore at her, and she didn't know how to help him. All she could do was listen.

"Well, my ex-wife, she didn't stick around for too long after she realized that the jet-setting way of life was over. She agreed to give up custody of Jamie since . . . he didn't fit into the lifestyle that she wanted for herself."

"And she married again?"

He nodded. "She married one of my teammates, a guy called Cole and carried on with her life. I carried on with mine. For years I was bitter about the whole experience. I didn't want to see her. I didn't want her to see my son. I forgot how much of an impact that would have on the boy. When he was about five, he asked me for the first time why it was that he didn't have a mother like the other kids did. I didn't know what to tell him. After that, I wrote to her, and I told her that I wanted her to be a part of the child's life. Well," and he massaged the area around his temples, "she basically told me that as far as she was concerned, she didn't have a son, and if I was starting to have trouble with the boy, and thought that I could now off-load him on her, she would fight me all the way through the courts."

Lola covered her mouth with a hand. "My God."

"Exactly," Chaz agreed. "So, after that, on his birthday, and at Christmas, I started sending him cards . . . made up to look like they came from her." His eyes glinted at her like black diamonds. "You should have seen him. He was so happy. So . . . excited to know that his mother had written to him. That he had a real-live mother and he wasn't different from the other kids."

Lola bent her head against his shoulder to hide the glimmer of tears in her eyes.

"Then just **out** of the blue, a few days ago, a real letter showed up. She's getting a divorce. And she wants to see Jamie."

Lola lifted her head. "Just like that?"

Chaz shrugged. "I wanted to give her the benefit of the doubt. But after all this time, and no contact at all, I had to wonder what she was up to."

Lola got up to open the bedroom door. She returned to sit.

"Thought I heard a sound from Jamie's room." Then, "Where does she live now? LA?"

"I think she's also got a place out in New York. A brownstone somewhere in Manhattan."

"So how is this all connected to Jamie getting sick?"

He flexed the stiffness from his knuckles and got up to pace. "I received another letter from her today, and . . . apparently, her plans have changed again. She won't be coming to see him after all."

"Ah," Lola said. "And you told Jamie this."

Chaz nodded. "He had a fit of screaming hysterics. Unusual for him, since he's always such a good kid."

Lola cleared her throat but decided to just leave it alone for right then.

"And the stomachache and so on followed?"

"Yes. Within about half an hour of me telling him this, he developed this stomach thing."

She stroked the back of Chaz's neck. "Well, you never know; she might change her mind and decide to come after all."

A frown settled in his eyes. "I wouldn't count on it."

Lola smiled at him. Maybe he wouldn't count on it, but she most certainly would.

"Why don't you try and get some sleep?" she said when she sensed that he was all talked out. "I'll sit up with Jamie."

He gave her a grateful look. "Are you sure?"

Lola nodded. "Sure."

Chapter Twenty-seven

It took two weeks of investigation for Lola to track down the exact whereabouts of Chaz's ex-wife, Veronica. She'd gone to a private eye and provided him with all the information she had. The woman's maiden name, married name, city of residence. And then she had sat back to wait.

The call came in on a Friday night just after a session of particularly spectacular lovemaking. Lola lay with her body draped over his, arm flung across chest, leg over leg, eyes half-closed, brain in a fog of satiation. And Chaz held her slightly damp body to his with both arms, his fingers moving with wonder over the shape of her shoulders, the long lines of her back, the curve of her smooth and very significant buttocks.

When the phone rang, he said in a vaguely irritated-sounding voice, "Who can be calling at this time?"

He had been anticipating turning her yet again onto the flat of her back and was not at all pleased by the untimely interruption of the buzzing phone.

Lola stirred, lifted a tousled head to peer at the caller ID, and then sat up. She moved so quickly that she very nearly wrenched a muscle in her back.

"I have to take this," she looked at him with apologetic eyes, "in private."

Chaz gave her a tight-jawed look as she scurried off to the bathroom wrapped in a long sheet and then closed the door behind herself. She picked up the wall phone and spoke softly into it.

"What've you got for me?"

The strident voice of Jimmy Mather came back. "It took a bit of doing, but I've got her."

"Where?" she whispered.

"Southern Cal. A place called Calabasas."

"You've got an address for me of course."

Jimmy Mather smiled. The fact that he had completed the job in under a month would mean a fat bonus check for him. He repeated the address while Lola scribbled it on a white pad. She read it back to him just to make sure that she had gotten it right; then she thanked him and hung up. What she was going to do would be done in utter and total secrecy. Chaz would not know about it until everything was arranged. And arrange things she would. She intended to be on the Saturday afternoon flight to Los Angeles. She would spend the weekend there. And, by Monday, Veronica would be accompanying her back to Maryland, even if she had to drag the woman kicking and screaming onto the next flight out.

She tore the piece of paper from the pad, folded it, and then tucked it carefully into one of the peach-colored vanity drawers in the bathroom. She then turned on the faucet and made an elaborate pretense of washing her face and hands. After a few minutes of this, she left the bathroom.

Chaz was lying on his back staring at the ceiling with an expression of brooding on his face. He turned toward her as soon as she reappeared.

"Who was that?"

"Business," she said.

And Lola got onto the foot of the bed and began crawling suggestively toward him. She slithered up the mattress, ducking beneath the sheet that now covered him from the waist down, and suddenly popping playfully out of the other end to say, "Boo."

But he was in no mood to play. "Was that your senator friend again?"

Lola blinked at him, genuinely surprised. "What? No. I told you it was just a business call."

"A business call, at . . . " he looked at his watch, "almost eleven-thirty at night?"

She sucked in a little breath. Jesus, he was getting possessive. He seemed to have completely forgotten the little rule about their each being free to pursue their own affairs. Not that she minded this, of course. It was a good thing, as far as she could see. It didn't mean that he loved her, though. Just that he didn't like to share. And that was better than nothing.

"What *was* that?" And he glared at her with hard suspicion in his eyes.

She touched his chest. "Are you upset?"

He took a while to answer that. "No. I'm not upset. But isn't this supposed to be our time? I hardly get a chance to see you during the day most days because of my work, your work. And—"

"It wasn't George Mason, I promise you," she interrupted.

His brows knitted. "Some other man then?"

"You're the only man I want," she hedged, hoping that he would relinquish the subject, just letting it go.

He was silent again, and she knew that he wasn't mollified. That somewhere deep within the recesses of his mind, he was turning over what she had just said, weighing it against everything else, and was coming up with something that she just wasn't doing.

She rested her chin on the elevated bend of his knee. Turned her face toward him so that her cheekbone lay against the joint.

"Chaz. Do you want a . . . different relationship with me?"

"Different?"

"More exclusive, I mean?"

He sighed, turned to face her. "You know this wasn't supposed to happen this way."

Lola held on to a smile. This was exactly the way she had hoped it would happen.

"What does that mean?" she pressed.

He turned her, parted her legs, and then slid his hands up the inner curves of her thighs. He stopped just short of his goal and a frustrated breath shuddered through her.

"It means that the good senator is out of the picture. You're not going to see him anymore."

"I'm . . . not?"

"You're not."

And he stroked the hidden nub of flesh with the tip of a finger and Lola opened to him, her legs trembling. He parted the wet folds with a thumb and used his finger to pleasure her. She bit down on her lower lip as intense waves of sensation hit her in tight unrelenting spasms. Her hand came down to hold his, and through lips that had gone strange and rubberlike, she managed, "You . . . I want you. Now."

He moved over her, balancing himself on his arms, nudging her wider with a leg. Lola closed her eyes as he entered her in one solid thrust. This was heaven, pure and simple. To have a man whose appetites exactly matched hers was simply . . .

She groaned as he continued to move with the same leisurely pace, and her hips lifted anxiously to urge him on. Her legs clawed at his back; her fingernails curled into his shoulders. But, with supreme strength, he held her steady and moved with calculated sloth until she was screaming at him, tearing at him. Then, when she could take no more of it, he gave her what she had needed all along. And she matched him thrust for thrust, her body surging upward to meet him, her head thrown backward, her mouth lolling open.

She was way beyond intelligible speech. She grunted as he did, uncaring of how she might appear, of what he might think. He bent his head into the curve of her neck, bit down on the warm flesh there. And she cried out to him, saying his name over and over and over again . . .

Lola boarded the mid-afternoon flight to Los Angeles. She was dressed in blue jeans, a matching light blue T-shirt, strappy blue sandals, sunglasses perched jauntily on her nose. Her hair cascaded about her shoulders in blue-black ringlets, and heads turned as she stepped onto the aircraft. She greeted a few of the passengers in the first-class cabin as she passed, smiling and nodding, asking after their wives. Then she buckled herself into her own seat, accepted a glass of perfectly chilled wine, and sat back to enjoy the flight.

An hour outside of Los Angeles, one of her fellow first-class passengers came over. He was a tall blond man with aquiline features and a smattering of gray at his temples. Lola looked up at him as his shadow settled over her. She'd been nose deep in the *New York Times*.

"Bill. Didn't see you when I got on. How're things on Wall Street?" She spoke casually to arguably one of the most influential and certainly one of the wealthiest CEOs in the investment banking business.

Bill Conley settled himself on an arm and smiled at Lola with shrewd green eyes.

"Taking a trip out to the Coast, are you? Another acquisition?"

Lola chuckled and folded her newspaper away. She passed the next half an hour chatting amiably about everything from the general business climate to the perfect time for skiing at Aspen. When the captain made his arrival announcement, she shook Conley's hand, promised to fit him in for lunch or dinner when she got back to the East Coast, and turned her mind to the task at hand. She was being met at the LAX airport by a car sent by the Four Seasons hotel. She would check into her suite first, get herself properly situated, and then give Veronica a call.

Lola glanced at her watch, and her mind drifted inevitably to Chaz. She had told him that she had business to take care of out in Los Angeles. He had given her a hard, suspicious look and then asked if she needed a ride to the airport. It had been a difficult maneuver getting out of that one, but she had managed to persuade him that she had already made arrangements for a car. He had seen her off with a kiss, a tight hug, and a promise that he would call her as soon as she got to her hotel. She had given him the number to her suite, because not to do so would have utterly convinced him that she was running off to Los Angeles for an illicit weekend with Senator Mason.

As soon as the plane had landed and taxied to the gate, she grabbed her low-slung handbag and walked briskly out to the VIP area where she was being met. The temperature was a beautiful seventy-eight degrees, with a brisk wind blowing in from the ocean. The fronds of the palm trees swayed slightly in the refreshing breeze, and Lola looked around her with great interest. Los Angeles. She loved the laid-back lifestyle. And one of these days she was going to buy a house somewhere on the ocean, leave the cold winters of the East permanently behind.

"Miss St. James?"

She turned. A man dressed in the characteristic tunic of the Four Seasons hotel was making his way toward her. She beamed in a friendly way at him and asked, "My driver?"

The man nodded. "Yes, ma'am. I've already got your luggage. Are you ready to go? The car's parked at the curb."

Lola followed the man back to the low-slung black limousine, climbed into its soft cream leather interior, and immediately picked up the phone. She called Annie first.

"I've just landed," Lola said as soon as the phone was picked up. "Has Camille called?"

Annie, who was staring through the back kitchen window at a pair of dangling ten-year-old legs, said, "She called just after you left. Said the reception venue's fallen through."

Lola sighed. "Annie, see what you can do to convince her to have the thing at the house. I mean, the grounds are big enough to accommodate at least five, six hundred people . . . maybe more. And I'm sure Chaz should be finished with the landscaping part of the project by September. A fall wedding outside would be nice, wouldn't it? We could put up tents, decorate everywhere . . ." She sighed with the thought of it. "It would be beautiful. And the weather should still be good."

"Uhm-hmm," Annie agreed, and then she left off to bellow, "Little boy, get down from there right now! Do you hear me? Don't make me come outside."

Lola covered the mouth of the phone and asked the driver, "How much longer to the hotel?"

"About forty-five minutes, give or take a few."

She nodded and thanked the man as Annie hollered in the background.

"Annie," she said now, "is the kid giving you trouble again?"

She heard something that sounded very much like a thud, and then Annie came back onto the phone to say, "Lola honey, I'm going to have to call you back. That boy, I don't know what it is, but he's tearing up the place again. I'll call you back." And she hung up.

Lola settled back in the seat. She knew what it was,

though. The reason for the child's uncontrollable behavior hadn't been clear before, but now she understood. It seemed that whenever his mother failed to
come through for him, he had one of his acting-out
sessions.

She closed her eyes for a second. Veronica was one
of the coldest women she had yet come across, but that
was perfectly all right, because she was very sure that
Chaz's ex-wife had never dealt with a woman like
her. . . .

Chapter Twenty-eight

The hotel was beautiful, but Lola hardly noticed it at all as she climbed from the back of the limousine. All the way over from the airport, her mind had been working. The reason for Veronica's negligence was something that she'd probably never fully understand. But whether she understood the woman's thinking or not was of no particular significance. What was important was that she get her to, at the very least, agree to spend some time with her son. A summer here, a Christmas there, was surely not too much to ask. Whatever had happened between her and Chaz was completely irrelevant and should not be taken out on the child. That would be wrong. And Lola intended to let the woman know this in no uncertain terms. The smooth skin creased between her brows. She would try the soft, reasonable approach first, but if that failed to work, she was perfectly willing to drop the ax in the most brutal way.

"Welcome to the Four Seasons, Miss St. James. Your suite is ready."

She gave the liveried attendant a brief smile and a, "Thank you."

She made small talk with the man on the way up in the nicely appointed elevator, assuring him that she had had an excellent flight out and that she was in Los Angeles for business and not pleasure.

Once she was settled in the two-story suite, she called Chaz's cellular phone, left a message saying that she was in Los Angeles, and then fished out her PDA. She dialed the number that the private detective had given her, kicked off her sandals, and then lay back on the bed with her toes digging into the soft pelt of blankets.

The phone rang several times before it was finally answered. A melodious-sounding female voice.

"Veronica?" Lola said without preamble.

There was a brief hesitation and then, "Yes. Who am I speaking to?"

Lola sat up. "My name is Lola St. James. I'm in Los Angeles for a few days, just over the weekend, actually, and I'd like us to meet."

The voice hardened by just a bit. "I'm sorry . . . I'm afraid I don't understand you."

"I have a matter I'd like to discuss. It has to do with your son, Jamie."

There was utter silence, and then without warning the phone went dead. A hard little smile came and went in Lola's eyes. OK. So she wanted to play hardball then. Well, that was fine. Perfectly fine.

Lola pressed the switch hook on the phone and when the concierge answered, said, "I'd like a car please. In five minutes."

Her clothes had already been unpacked and hung neatly in one of the bedroom closets. And Lola changed quickly, exchanging her jeans and T-shirt for a pair of cream cotton slacks and a dandelion yellow shirt. She snapped on earrings, a matching necklace, and a pair of tan patent-leather pumps, ran a comb through her raven locks, spent a moment touching up her lipstick, and then stepped from the suite with the beginnings of fire in her eyes.

"Forty-six Vacasa Circle," she told the driver. "It's somewhere in Calabasas."

And then she sat back with legs crossed and sunglasses on her nose. From time to time she glanced out the window at the passing scenery, her gaze settling every so often on the smooth glass face of one corporation headquarters or another. She made mental notes as they sped along the freeway. It had been at least six months since she had made any acquisitions, nothing had really caught her fancy in all that time, but she had been considering primarily midsize East Coast concerns. Maybe once she got back to Maryland and things with Chaz and Jamie were properly settled, she'd turn her mind back to the corporate jungle.

"Forty-eight Vacasa did you say, miss?" the driver asked as they crossed the border from Los Angeles to Ventura County.

Lola leaned forward. "Forty-six."

They passed a few more exits and then coasted down the ramp for Vacasa Circle Drive.

"I think it's one of those gated communities," the driver said, glancing in the rearview mirror at his passenger.

Lola nodded at him. OK. Well, she would just have to use her cunning to get inside if that was the case.

The driver slowed the car as they came to a pair of wrought-iron gates and then came to a complete stop at the guard hut. He wound down his window and said, "Forty-six Vacasa."

The guard checked his clipboard, came out to the car, and bent low to examine the occupants.

Lola wound down her window, stuck her head out, and said very pleasantly, "I'm here for the open house."

The guard came over to her window. "There is no open house today, ma'am. I think you must be—"

"No," Lola interrupted. "I'm not mistaken. I just flew in from the East Coast today for a private showing and this is just not acceptable." She snapped her fingers. "I want to speak to your supervisor."

The man swallowed and darted a glance toward the phone in the hut.

"Who did you say you were again, ma'am?"

"Lola St. James."

The man looked at the phone again. "Not *the* Lola St. James? The one who was just on the cover of this week's *Newsweek*?"

She adjusted her sunglasses. "Yes, I think that cover should be out by now." She gave her watch a glance. "I really don't have a lot of time. If you'd like to check with—"

The guard waved her suggestion away with, "No, no. I don't think it'll be a problem. In fact, it's an honor to meet you, ma'am. Please go through." And he went back to the hut to open the gates.

Lola sucked in a breath and then released it slowly. The fact that the guard had recognized her had been a stroke of luck. Things could just as easily have gone the other way entirely.

The road curved smoothly to the left and then bent again in the opposite direction. Lola wound the window down all the way and let the wind whip through the car. She had to admit, it was a nice little community. Neatly manicured lawns, tasteful pieces of stone sculpture, red and white miniature rosebushes. And each house sat on at least half an acre of land. There were a few whitewashed eighteenth-century colonials, excellent replicas of Tuscan villas, ultramodern cabin houses with thick wooden faces and darkly tinted convex windows. And forming a jagged semicircle somewhere off in the distance was a towering line of red and gold mountains.

Lola shook her head. So this was what Veronica had given up her son for? An immaculate little community of houses? A millionaire lifestyle? What a superficial piece of—

The driver's voice broke into her train of thought. "I think this is the one, miss. Would you like me to call the house phone, let them know you're here?"

Lola pushed a flyaway curl behind an ear. "No. I'll just ring the bell."

She climbed from the car as soon as it had come to a complete stop. The house was on a slight rise, very close to the curb, with red hewn stone stairs leading all the way up to the front doors. On either side of the stairs was a long and well-maintained ramp.

Lola walked briskly up the run of stairs and placed a very determined finger on the bell.

She heard the sound of footsteps and mentally prepared herself for battle. The door was pulled back and a short, conservatively dressed woman with a round face and kind eyes said, "Yes? Can I help you?"

Lola removed her sunglasses. She knew instinctively that this was not Veronica Simms-Cole.

"I'm here to see Miss Cole."

The woman smiled. "Oh. How nice. She hardly ever gets visitors. Come in. Come in."

Lola entered and her eyes swept the comfortably furnished living room. She hadn't expected it to be this easy, but she was absolutely certain that what was to come would make up for all of that.

"Would you have a seat? I'll let her know you're here." The little woman walked off through an archway and then returned to say, "Your name. I forgot it . . . or did I ask you at all?"

Lola smiled at her. "I'd like it to be a surprise, if that's OK with you?"

The woman gave her a very pleased look. She loved surprises.

"I'll get her. Won't be a minute. Would you like something to drink while you wait? Maybe a soda? Fruit juice? Water?"

Lola assured her that she was fine and settled back to wait on a comfortable floral print sofa. She occupied herself with looking around the sitting room. It was nicely done in warm desert tones. There were flowers on tables, all housed in beautiful fluted vases. Throw cushions tossed around here and there. Pictures arranged on the mantelpiece.

Pictures.

Lola got up to have a look. Somehow she had not imagined that a woman like Veronica would have had any use for something as sentimental as photographs.

She picked up a gilt-edged frame. It held the picture of a stunningly beautiful woman holding up a fish and laughing heartily at the camera. Lola replaced the frame. She hadn't changed much since high school.

Lola went down the short line of photographs and then paused at the end. There was a picture of an infant all done up in a knit cap and a fuzzy white jumper. She picked up the frame and almost dropped it when a voice behind her said, "Would you mind coming out to the pool? She's having one of her days."

Lola replaced the heavy frame. One of her days, indeed. The woman was absolutely unbelievable.

"I'm the housekeeper, by the way," the woman said as she walked Lola out through open French doors and onto a slab stone patio.

Lola smiled, nodded, but her eyes were already on the glittering blue of the pool. There was someone seated there beneath one of the large green and white umbrellas.

She gritted her teeth. What a woman. She knew that she had a guest, and she couldn't even make the effort to get out of her chair and meet her halfway. Well, she was going to receive a tongue-lashing the likes of which she had never received before.

"Ronnie," the housekeeper said as soon as they were close enough. "This young lady has dropped by to see you."

Veronica Simms-Cole looked up, her face partially shaded by the large brim of a white hat. She smiled at the housekeeper and then waved Lola into a facing chair.

"I guess you're from the real estate office? You've come about the house. . . ."

Lola sat, waited for the housekeeper to disappear back indoors, and then in a very hard voice leaned forward to say, "I spoke to you on the phone earlier. I think we were having some problems with the line, because quite soon into our conversation we seemed to lose our connection."

The woman's jaw sagged and then she looked around wildly.

"I have nothing to say to you. Why have you come here to my house? You have to leave. You must leave." And she reached for the phone that sat on the poolside table.

Lola shifted the phone away, her eyes glittering like twin daggers.

"Look, lady," she began, and then the words she had been about to say dwindled and dried in her throat. Her eyes flashed up to the woman's face and glanced over the glimmer of wet in her eyes.

"Yes," Veronica said in a brittle little voice. "Go ahead. You can say it. I guess Chaz sent you here. Well, have a good look so you can report back to him everything you've seen." And she removed the blanket that until now had been covering her legs.

Lola looked down at the shriveled legs. "You're disabled," she said.

Veronica tilted her chin. "The doctors have said that I might walk again. It's not necessarily permanent." She wiped the trickle of a tear away from the side of her face.

Lola pressed her lips together. "How long?"

"Six and a half years."

Lola looked at the legs again. "Six and a half years? You've been unable to walk for six and a half years?"

The woman sniffled. "I know what you think. I'm a terrible mother. But," and she wiped another tear away, "the doctors have said that my paralysis is only temporary . . . that I'll walk again. And I don't want my boy to see me like this." She patted at her nose with a handkerchief. "I want him to know me as I was. I can walk again. I know I can." She pounded a hand against her legs. "But they just refuse to do anything I want. They won't move at all. Not even a little."

She began to cry now, and Lola widened her eyes. She had been prepared for just about anything, but not this.

She reached forward to gently pat the other woman's hand.

"Should I get someone? Would you like something to drink?"

Veronica snuffled into her handkerchief and then looked up at Lola with red-rimmed eyes.

"Do you think every day of my life for the last decade I haven't wanted to hold my child in my arms? But how can I hold him with these legs?" She swallowed and then continued in a broken manner. "And Chaz . . . I don't want him to know about this . . . this . . . problem." She waved a hand. "I want him to remember me as I was. I don't want his pity. I can deal with just about anything he has to give me, anything but that."

Lola let her cry for a while longer. In a way, she actually pitied the woman. Not because of her infirmity, but because she didn't possess the wisdom to understand that in the eyes of her son, she would never be crippled, never be less than absolutely perfect.

"Veronica," she said as gently as she could manage. "Jamie needs you. He's just a little boy, and he doesn't understand any of this . . . All he knows is that his mother doesn't want him . . . his mother doesn't care for him. And that's not true. Is it?"

Red-rimmed eyes were trained on her again. "Is that what Chaz told you? That I don't want him?" She sucked in a trembling breath. "I know I left him all alone with Chaz back in those early crazy days, but I always meant to come back for him. I always meant that. But then there was the accident and . . . and . . ."

Lola gripped the hand that she was still holding. "Your second husband left you after the accident?"

Veronica nodded, shrugged. "He stuck around for maybe a year. But after that . . ." She swallowed and tried to steady her breathing. "I didn't want Chaz to know about my divorce then, because of how we had parted." She looked off into the distance, turned back to look at Lola with sorrow-filled eyes. "We were just young stupid kids in those days. We should never have gotten married. Don't really know why we did." She gave a husky laugh. "He was always talking about Sadie Green. It used to make me so mad in the beginning. It was always Sadie this, Sadie that. I came to hate the girl."

Lola sat back in her chair. Her hands were cold and trembling. He had been thinking about her even then?

When she was calm enough, she asked, "Why did

you send a letter just a few weeks ago asking to see Jamie if you knew that there was no chance that you would ever let him see you like this?"

"I went to see another doctor. A specialist in New York. He said that my spinal cord was intact. No damage. That I should be able to walk. So the next day, when I was still feeling happy and positive, I sent off the letter to Washington, D.C."

Lola nodded. "He was so excited about it. You can't imagine how much. And when he learnt that you didn't want to see him after all. . ."

Veronica made a moaning noise and hid her face in her hands. "I've made a mess of my life," she said. "An absolute mess of it. The only thing I had going for me was my looks. And for the last six years, I haven't even had that."

Lola leaned forward. "Look. Life is hard. There's no doubt about that at all. But, as I see it, you have one of two choices. Either you continue doing as you have done for the past six years—you let your son grow to adulthood thinking that you abandoned him and couldn't care less about him—or . . ." she paused to let the first option sink in, "or . . . you can take this first bold step. Reach out to him. Let him know that you care. Call him on the phone maybe. Just so he can hear your voice."

Veronica shook her head. "No. I can't do that. He'll want to come out to visit if I start calling him. And then Chaz will start pressuring me. I just can't do it. I can't."

Lola stood. "You *can* do it. You *know* you can do it.

I know you can do it. It's a choice, Veronica. And life is all about making them. Good ones. Bad ones. Make a good one this time." She pulled out a business card, scribbled her phone number at the Four Seasons on the back of it.

"I'm going to be in town until Monday. You can reach me at this number."

The remainder of the weekend passed quickly. Lola spent most of it indoors. She spoke to Chaz for a long while on the phone as soon as she returned from Calabasas. And for the first time since they had begun their relationship, he told her that he missed her. She sat on the bed cradling the phone close to her cheek and considered for one brief wild impetuous minute flying him out so that he might spend the remaining days with her. But as much as she might want it, she knew that it wasn't possible. So instead, she contented herself with long telephone conversations and multiple cold showers.

She spent the day on Sunday sitting out on the balcony sipping lemonade and flipping through the latest paperback best seller. Every time the phone rang, her heart jumped. But as the hours rolled from Sunday evening on into Monday, it became clear that Veronica was not going to call.

She called Veronica again just before she stepped out of the suite on Monday and was surprised when the woman actually took her call.

"Veronica," she said, "I'm going to make a deal with you." And she outlined the arrangement that she had in mind, explaining who she was and what medical resources she would be able to put at Veronica's disposal.

"First thing is, though, I want you to call the child at least once a week, every week from now on. That's non-negotiable. If you agree to do that, I promise you that not only will I fly one of the world's leading spinal injury specialists out to you by the end of this very week, but I also personally will move heaven and earth to ensure that if it is possible for you to walk again, you will walk again. Deal?" she asked into the little pit of silence.

"But how do I know you'll keep your end of the bargain? And why should you anyway? What do you get out of it?"

"I get nothing but Jamie's happiness. His father's happiness. And you can take my word on that to the bank." Lola allowed that to sink in and then pushed home her advantage. "An offer like this one will probably never come your way again, Veronica. Take it. You can only win."

There was another silence, and then in a soft little voice she said, "OK."

Chapter Twenty-nine

Chaz had passed the entire weekend on the property. He had taken care of the usual household chores, the cooking, cleaning, seeing to the laundry. But none of the activity had calmed him. Just the night before, he had spent many sweaty hours wrapped in dreams of Lola. But he had not been the man with her. He had struggled hard to see the face of her lover, and when he had, he had woken himself with hoarse, unintelligible words. He had passed the remainder of the night lying on the flat of his back, staring up at the spackled white ceiling, unwilling to sleep lest the dreams claimed him again. He had considered calling her then, just to make sure that she was alone, but had discarded the idea almost as soon as it had come into his head. It was ridiculous how much he wanted her. And it wasn't just the sex anymore. It had been weeks since he had even attempted to pan off the deep and very puzzling feelings he had for her on the great physical relationship they both shared. He hadn't intended for any of this to happen. But life sometimes, and he knew this better than most people, had a way of throwing curves.

He lifted the curtain now and stared out at the darkness. She had told him that she would be back no later than midnight. It was now almost twelve-thirty, and despite the fact that he knew that she was well able to take care of herself, he worried.

Chaz flipped on the TV and forced himself to scan the news channels. His heart beat heavily in his chest as he went from one to the next. Good. Good. No news of problems with any airlines. That was good then. It meant that she was just late. Possibly the plane had been delayed. Or maybe she had missed her original flight. Or she could have gotten mugged on the way to the airport. Jesus.

He stood and wiped a hand across his face. Maybe he should call the airline just to check. He had her flight number. It would just be a simple matter of . . . His eyes flashed to the driveway. Headlights. Thank God.

Lola climbed from the interior of the car, thanked the driver, and then slung her large carry-on bag across her shoulder.

"I'll take that."

She turned with happy eyes and barely managed not to fling herself directly into Chaz's arms. He stood before her with a slight smile twisting his lips, and she touched him lightly on the arm and said in a bemused manner, "You waited up for me?"

"Of course." He took her shoulder bag and then the large department store bag that she had set at her feet. She smiled at him.

"Things for Jamie, and maybe a little something for you."

He cocked an eyebrow at her, and his eyes gleamed with mysterious lights in the semi-darkness. "You mean you remembered me all the way out there in LA?"

And they joked back and forth all the way into the

house. Annie was wrapped in a bathrobe, halfway down the stairs, when Lola pushed the front door open.

"Annie," Lola said with the beginnings of concern in her voice. "You shouldn't have waited up for me." She glanced at her watch. "It's after twelve-thirty."

Annie wrapped her robe about her a bit tighter and said with sparkling eyes, "Do you think I'm old and falling apart? Come here and give me a hug."

Lola went, pressing kisses to both sides of Annie's face. It was great to be home, and she had managed to accomplish what she had gone out to Los Angeles to do.

Chaz stood at the bottom of the stairs looking at the two women, and Annie whispered into Lola's ear, "I'd better get on back up to bed. You'll tell me what happened tomorrow."

"Come on up," Lola said to him as soon as Annie had disappeared around the bend of the corridor. And then she wrinkled her nose and said, "Jamie must be asleep by now. So you have to get back."

Chaz bent to pick up the shopping bag. "Jamie's on a sleepover at a friend's house."

Lola beamed at him and held out a hand for his. They walked hand in hand up the stairs and into her suite, where Chaz placed the bags on the floor, locked the door behind them, and then beckoned her with a, "Come here, you."

Lola went, with warm breath in her throat. It was so good to see him again. So very good to be back. His arms wrapped around her, and she met his eyes.

"Chaz, I've been thinking."

He bent his head to kiss one side of her mouth. "What have you been thinking?"

Warmth curled through her and Lola struggled to remain focused. "Jamie needs a change of scenery."

Chaz kissed the other side of her mouth and gave a considered, "Uhm."

Lola swallowed. "Yes. And I'd like us . . . all of us to spend maybe . . ." He kissed her again, and this time Lola seized his bottom lip and ran her tongue over the curve of it. ". . . two weeks in Bermuda."

He lifted his head, stared at her. "Bermuda?"

She nodded. "Bermuda. I've a villa there. Right on the beach. We could leave this coming weekend, take Annie . . . It would be great. Jamie would love it. Beautiful weather, beautiful beach . . ."

Chaz sighed. "You know I can't just pick up and go. What about all of the work I'm doing here?"

"You have a foreman now. Doesn't he oversee things for you?"

"Yes, but—"

"The child needs it," Lola interrupted. "Haven't you noticed that he's been acting up just a little bit more than usual?"

"He has. That's true. For the first time in a good long while I came very close to giving him a spanking. Mrs. Lewis saved him from it. That's why I sent him off to spend a night with one of his friends. I know the family well. I figured that all of this time spent around the place wasn't helping him any."

Lola removed herself from his arms, went to sit on the bed, bent to remove her shoes.

"You know why his behavior's taken a turn for the worse all of a sudden, don't you?"

Chaz came to sit beside her. "His mother. I know."

Lola rubbed a consoling hand across the back of his neck.

"I have a feeling everything's going to work out, but in the meantime," and she gave him a bright gamin-like grin, "let's take his mind off things by taking him down to my villa. He'll have a blast there. He'll be able to play in the sand, in the water, explore the place. It'll be so much fun for a little boy, and it might take his mind off his mother. What do you think?"

Chaz removed one of her earrings and then the other.

"I'll tell you what I think in the morning."

She lay back on the bed and he reached forward to slowly unbutton her shirt.

"I'm going to massage and kiss every tired, every sore, every forgotten muscle in your body."

Lola chuckled. "Uhm-hmm?"

He kissed the bend of her neck, lifted her chin to kiss the crease there.

"That's right. And when I'm finished with those, I'm going to start on the non-muscular parts . . . and you know what I'm going to do to those?"

Lola gave a little shriek as he bent his head to nip the side of her rib cage. She laughed heartily as his fingers came up to tickle.

"What're you going to do?"

He pressed a kiss to her navel, sucked the skin into his mouth.

"You're going to have to wait and see, girl."

The remainder of the night was passed with limbs intertwined, sheets tangled and hanging, mouths locked together, until finally, in the dim light of morning, they both slept, exhausted.

It was the first morning that Lola had ever awoken in his arms, and she did so slowly, opening first one eye and then the other. He was completely wrapped about her, one long leg thrown across the curve of her thigh, an arm nestled in the center of her back. His head rested against the curve of an arm and he slept soundlessly, his face relaxed and peaceful.

Lola turned with care and reached across the short expanse of mattress for the phone. She had turned off the ringer before leaving for California, but the blinking of the light on the dial told her that it was ringing.

"Yes," she said in a voice still husky with sleep. She rubbed a hand across her eyes, pushed a few curls back to lie behind an ear. "What was that now?" she asked, and the sleep left her by degrees.

Bob O'Brien repeated himself. He had been Lola St. James's primary lawyer for the past fifteen years and he knew her likes, dislikes, pet peeves, and idiosyncrasies. And one major pet peeve of hers was that bad news should always be delivered to her the very first thing in the morning.

Lola sat up, taking care not to wake Chaz, who was still sound asleep beside her. "She wants more money? How much more?"

Bob O'Brien cleared his throat. "I believe the figure she mentioned was about a half a million dollars."

Lola laughed softly into the phone. "A half a million dollars? Is she out of her mind? Tell her that I won't pay it. And also let her know that if I receive any more of these ridiculous demands, I will sever the arrangement between us. No more money. Not a cent."

Bob O'Brien made the appropriate placatory sounds: "I'll pass on your feelings, of course, but she says to tell you that she knows all about Sadie Green and should you not pay, she will go to Chaz Kelly about it." He paused briefly and then pressed on. "None of it made any particular kind of sense to me actually, but she said that you would understand exactly what she meant."

Lola's jaw clenched. Audrey Mackenzie. The woman was a thorn in her flesh. But Lola wouldn't be blackmailed. She would take away all of Audrey's presumed power by telling Chaz herself. She should have done so a long while ago. But she had let the foolishness drag on until it had been so hard to tell him that she had just left it alone. But now, regardless of what happened, she would tell him.

"Tell Audrey for me," her voice developed a hard edge, ". . . that Chaz already knows. And help her understand that I value integrity in everything that I do, so another stunt like this, and the money will stop."

"What will you stop?" Chaz muttered, and he opened black opal eyes and stared directly at her.

Lola covered the mouthpiece with a hand and said, "My lawyer, Bob O'Brien. You haven't met him yet, but you will tomorrow. I thought we could have a little dinner party with some of my friends. Have you met Camille?"

She went back to the phone and to Bob, who was saying, "Hello?" repeatedly in her ear. "I'll finalize everything with you later today, OK, Bob?" And she hung up before the confused man could say anything more.

She looked at Chaz with slightly guilty eyes and he said in a gravelly voice, "That wasn't your lawyer, was it?"

Lola blinked. "It was." She leaned down, kissed him flush on the mouth. "It was. His name is Robert O'Brien."

She took a preparatory breath. There was no time like the present. So she would do it now, before she could talk herself out of telling him again.

"Chaz . . ."

He propped an arm beneath his head. "I'll go to Bermuda . . . but . . ." He gave her a lopsided smile. "I have conditions."

Lola wet her lips. Oh lord. Conditions. Why couldn't she ever get anything at all without conditions?

"Which ones now?" Whatever they were, she had a strong feeling that they were going to put her in even more of a twist than she was currently in.

He laughed and dragged her down to lie with him. "Don't look so serious about it. I was only kidding." He feathered the bridge of her nose with kisses. "What I meant was, I want to take care of the costs for you, Annie, everyone."

Lola's eyebrows lifted, and for some unexplainable reason a rush of tears clustered in the backs of her eyes. She turned her head slightly, so that he didn't see the emotion in her eyes. But he caught her chin with tender fingers and said with worry in his voice, "You're crying."

"No," Lola choked. She was just touched. Deeply, deeply touched by the simple gesture that he had made. She knew that he couldn't really afford to pay for them all, but still, he had offered.

He stroked away the bead of moisture at the corner of her eye.

"Don't cry," he said in a tender voice, and he tucked her head beneath his chin.

Lola held back a sniffle. How could she tell him now? It would ruin everything. Their entire vacation. Why was her life always so darned complicated?

"Chaz, what would you do if you found your high school friend . . . Sadie again?"

She felt the muscles beneath her cheek tighten. "I'd be happy to see her again of course."

He smiled at her. "Have you been trying to find her? To surprise me?"

Lola pressed her lips together. Did she have a surprise for him. And he was going to hate her for it. He was never, ever going to forgive her. And whatever little bit of feeling he had developed towards her over the past weeks and months would be wiped out by her one single admission.

"I mean . . . what if Sadie had . . . say, changed her identity or something like that? So that you couldn't recognize her?"

His brow wrinkled. "Changed her identity?" And he gave a bark of laughter. "Now, that's really reaching, Lola St. James."

"But what if you never find her again?" she pressed. "Would that be a big deal?"

He shrugged. "All that history between us was a long time ago. I've already come to terms with the idea that I'll probably never see her again. I'm OK with that now." His eyes got playful again. "But what's all this about Sadie? Are you suddenly feeling threatened by an eighteen-year-old memory?"

"Threatened? No. Of course not." And Lola forced herself to laugh, too. She should really just blurt it out. Tell him right now who she was. But he wouldn't understand. She knew that now. And how could they go off to Bermuda if he wasn't even speaking to her anymore? No, she would tell him after they got back. Right after. She would just walk up to him, sit him down somewhere, and say, "Remember that Sadie Green person we were talking about that day? Well, you're looking at her." And then she would just have to deal with the fallout of that, much as she always did.

She sucked in a tight little breath. She had gotten herself into this ridiculous mess, so now she would just have to deal with it.

"So about Bermuda . . . when will we go?"

Chapter Thirty

Veronica called about an hour before they were ready to leave for the airport. Chaz was standing in the middle of the living room of the guesthouse, surrounded by several duffel bags and a large rollaway suitcase. Lola breezed through the front door with a bright, "Everyone ready to go?" just as the house phone began to ring.

Chaz hoisted a bag to his shoulder and hollered to Jamie, who had disappeared somewhere outside, "Jamie, I told you to come in and help with these bags!"

Chaz gave Lola a quick hug and then walked across to pick up the phone to say a very abrupt, "Yes? Hello?"

Lola watched as the bag slipped slowly down his shoulder to the bend in his arm, and her brain flashed through the possibilities as he said, "What? Who's calling?"

He turned, looked at her, covered the mouth of the receiver, and said, "My ex-wife. She wants to speak to Jamie. I don't believe it."

Lola felt the blood slowly warm her cheeks. It was so very nice to do good things for the ones you cared about.

"Your ex-wife?" she said, and she smiled at him with what she hoped was the appropriate degree of surprise. "Imagine that. Should I get him?"

Chaz placed the phone against the crook of his neck. "I don't know if that's such a good idea right now. That woman is unpredictable at best, and I really don't want her upsetting Jamie just before we have to get onto a plane."

Lola's eyes widened. What? Not after all she'd gone through to bring this about. Not talk to Jamie? Was he completely serious?

"I don't think speaking to his mother is likely to upset him," Lola coaxed. "Actually, I think it'll be a good thing. A very good thing. Just what the boy needs right now." She rubbed Chaz's arm. "Come on. Let me get him."

He sighed, rubbed a hand across the back of his neck. "I hope you're right about this."

Lola beamed. Of course she was right about it. She went to the front door and called, "Jamie? Jamie?"

The little boy came running, the side of his T-shirt and half of his jeans streaked with mud. Lola took him by the shoulder, turned him. "What have you been doing?"

He looked up at her, gave her a toothy grin. "Playing with the neighbor's dog."

"Come on then. Someone wants to speak to you."

His eyes widened. "To me? Where?" And he looked about the sitting room as though he expected someone to suddenly spring from behind a couch.

His father beckoned him over, handed him the phone. "Say hello to your, ah . . . mother." He hated calling her that, but the woman had carried and birthed the boy.

Jamie's eyes flashed from Lola to his father and then back to Lola.

"Is it a trick?" he asked in a little voice.

Lola swallowed. She was going to start crying in a minute. She stooped, cuddled the little body that had gone suddenly stiff.

"No, sweetie, it's not a trick. Your mother called specially to speak to you. Isn't that great?"

She handed him the phone but still continued to hold him as he said a very tentative, "Hello? Mama? . . . Yes, it's Jamie."

The flight across to Bermuda was a mere two-hour stretch and Jamie spent most of the trip running from one side of the plane to the next until Annie was finally forced to say, "Jamie boy, come and sit beside me; you're driving the other passengers crazy."

Lola held in a chuckle. The child had been practically bouncing off the walls since his brief telephone conversation with his mother. She had never seen such excitement. At first he had spoken in a stilted manner, only answering with a string of yes and no responses. But that hadn't lasted for very long. Not very far into the conversation, he had suddenly let loose with a barrage of questions. Where was she? What was she doing? Did she live in Hollywood? Was she close to Ice Cube's house? The questions were endless, and Chaz was finally forced to take the phone from him with the explanation that if they didn't leave right then, there was a very good chance that they would miss their flight.

Chaz had locked up the place, left phone numbers and very detailed instructions with the man he had placed in charge of things, and then they had all piled into Chaz's truck and headed off for the airport.

It had been years since Lola had flown anything other than first-class, but she settled into a window seat in economy class and tried not to notice how very tight the seats were beside and before her. Chaz was paying for the entire trip, and the very last thing that she wanted to do was make him think that she didn't appreciate everything that he was doing.

Lola pointed down at a strip of land now as the island came into view.

"Look, Jamie. There's Bermuda. See that little spot right there? That's where we're going to land."

Jamie clambered over his father, and Lola lifted him onto her lap. The child's eyes rounded, and then he turned to say in a very worried voice, "But it's too small. We'll never fit."

Chaz chuckled. "Don't worry, sport, it only looks that way."

Lola directed his attention to a large white cloud that seemed to suddenly wrap itself around one of the wings.

"See, we're going down now."

Jamie craned his neck. "How can you tell?"

"Look at the clouds, and the land. You'll see everything will start getting a lot closer. See the ocean?" She pointed at the large expanse of blue water. Jamie pressed his nose against the glass and asked with great excitement in his voice, "Will we be able to swim in it? Will there be any sharks?"

Lola kept him perfectly entertained all the way down and through customs. Since they were all American citizens, they whizzed right through the customs process and were outside standing on the concrete pavement in next to no time.

Chaz wrapped an arm about Lola's shoulders, and a feeling of happiness and contentment settled deep within her. This was life. *This* was what it was really all about.

"Mrs. Lewis, let me carry that bag for you," Chaz said now, as Annie heaved a particularly large carry-on bag to her shoulder.

"Nonsense." Annie waved him away. "Don't you have enough luggage to take care of yourself?"

Lola rolled her eyes at Chaz and whispered, "Let her do it. You'll never hear the end of it if you don't."

They all trundled off to a large old-fashioned American car that had been waiting for them at the curb, greeted the driver warmly, and then sat back to enjoy the trip as the salty air whipped through the car.

Under cover of a basket that now sat atop Annie's lap, one that she had absolutely refused to part with, she reached out to give Lola's hand an encouraging squeeze and a nod. Annie had noticed the very warm and attentive way in which Chaz had been treating Lola and, as far as she was concerned, it was a very good thing. A very good thing.

"Look, there's the villa." Lola pointed now at a beautiful white house that sat on a grassy swell just slightly above Mangrove Bay.

Chaz leaned out the window and let the wind hit him squarely in the face. "God, it's beautiful here." He sucked in a breath. "Why would anyone want to live anywhere else? You've got the ocean, the great weather, the people."

"Uhmm," Lola agreed. The very thought had occurred to her any number of times before, and one of the main reasons why she had never considered living in Bermuda full-time was now seated right beside her.

She looked down at the little boy who was literally bouncing up and down on the old cracked leather seats.

"You know, Jamie, the sands here are completely pink. Did you know that?"

And all the way up the little black tar road that led to the villa, Lola gave them all a running history on why that was so. She explained how the crushed shells of various sea creatures, mixed with the powdery fine delicate pink coral, combined to create the beautiful peachy pink sands. But at the end of her explanation Jamie gave her his version of ten-year-old skepticism, telling her flatly that he refused to believe any of it until he had seen it for himself. Because, as far as he was concerned, pink sands made no sense whatsoever.

Chaz exchanged a laughing glance with her, and Lola said, "Well, that puts me right in my place, doesn't it?"

The big car swept beneath a white latticework arbor covered with a profusion of creeping vines and red, yellow, and blue hibiscus and then came to a stop directly before the open front door.

Jamie scrabbled for the door handle, clambering over multiple arms and legs in his haste to get out. Annie, who had had quite a tiring trip and was nearing the very end of her tether, gave him a quick swat on the behind and a, "Sit still until everyone gets out of the car. I know you have better manners than that."

Lola clambered out first and was greeted by the resident housekeeper and cook.

"Welcome back to the Maison, Miss St. James. A hot towel for you?"

And the tall, slender woman went very efficiently around handing out hot towels.

Chaz wiped his hands and face and then did the same to Jamie, who had already dropped his towel to the ground.

"Can I go down to the beach, Dad? Can I?"

Chaz grabbed ahold of an arm and propelled Jamie through the doorway. "A little control now, Jamie. We're going to be here for two whole weeks. Just take it easy."

Lola linked arms with Chaz and Jamie. "Let's go freshen up first. Maybe have a little snack and then off to the beach." She looked at her watch. "It's still early. What do you think, Mister Jamie?"

Jamie whooped in response, pulled his arm away, and went pelting into the house with Annie hot on his trail.

"Let him go," Lola said as Chaz called after him in alarm. "I have truly never come across a child with so much energy."

Chaz nodded. "Too much energy sometimes."

"Come," Lola said, and she took him by the hand. "Let me show you the rest of the place."

There were three floors. Six bedrooms, each one air-conditioned and self-contained with its own toilet and shower. There was a library filled with everything from the latest Terri MacMillan best sellers to huge tomes on the theory of finance. There was a roof deck, two dining rooms, a sitting room on each floor, multiple breezy wraparound verandas, and in the center of it all, on the very first floor of the house, a large pool and Jacuzzi.

"And this," Lola said, opening up a door that led into a very spacious bedroom on the sea side of the villa, "is your room and—"

Chaz caught her about the waist and walked her back into a corner by the door. "My room?" he growled, nipping at the sides of her neck. "What do you mean by that, woman? Aren't we sharing a room?"

Lola gave his rump a playful slap. "I've already thought of that, young man, and . . ." She slipped from under his arm and danced into the middle of the room.

He followed. "And?"

She grinned at him. "And there's a certain method to my madness. See that door?"

Chaz took a look at the door she was pointing at. "I see it."

"Well," she said chirpily, "it leads directly into my room. So you can maintain your sense of decency and at the same time . . ." She wiggled her eyebrows.

Chaz grabbed her by the waist and pulled her back against him. "Decency be damned," he growled in her ear. "Tonight, we're going to get freaky right down in the sand."

The breath shuddered in Lola's chest. "Tonight?"

He bit the lobe of her ear. "Tonight."

The rest of the day passed swiftly. First they partook of a Bermudan midafternoon meal of stewed codfish, black-eyed peas, and rice, topped off with sweet baby potatoes and cassava pie. Then, wrapped in thick bath towels with Chaz armed with three large beach, umbrellas, they set off to spend the remainder of the day on the beach.

Jamie ran off ahead, despite the calls of his father to be careful and, before Lola and Chaz could even walk down the wooden stairs onto the pink sand beach, had stripped down to his swimming gear, and was dodging the waves as they came crashing ashore.

Lola took the boy out on a Jet Ski and spent the better part of the afternoon tearing back and forth across a small bay, with Jamie clinging to her middle, hollering for all he was worth.

Later, as the sun began to sink low in the sky, Annie came out to collect Jamie, and once they were alone, Lola cuddled into Chaz's arms on a long beach lounger and watched the glorious play of colors as they streaked their way across the darkening sky. Chaz stroked a hand slowly down the flat of her back, and Lola sighed in utter contentment as the gold of evening gave way to red and then flame-etched indigo. It was beautiful. Life was beautiful.

Chaz shifted her chin, and as naturally as though it had always been this way, they kissed. Softly, tenderly, and then with increasing passion. Her tongue mating with his, thrusting and darting, tasting, touching, stroking until they were both out of breath and panting.

He held her face between the palms of his two hands

and rubbed a thumb across the passion-swollen flesh of her mouth.

"I'm so glad you're here with me."

Lola straddled him with a leg. "How glad are you?" But he didn't respond the way she had thought he would to her teasing.

Instead, he rolled her completely into his arms and asked in a very serious manner, "Lola, did you really intend to marry that Mason guy?"

She stroked a finger across her nose, considered lying about it for a second.

"No. Not once . . . once our relationship had really gotten going."

His chest moved as though he'd been holding on to the breath.

"I want you to think carefully about what I'm about to ask you. It's something I never thought . . . Well, I just didn't expect it to ever happen to me again." He laughed, looked away for a second, looked back at her with intent eyes. "What I'm trying to say is, when we get back to the States, there's something I'm going to want to ask you. And how you answer will affect the rest of my life . . . your life. No, don't answer yet. I know I've sprung this on you . . . Hell, I don't even know how to process it myself. But think about it, and once we get back to the States . . . I'll ask you again in the proper way. OK?"

Lola nodded numbly. Throughout his little speech, she had gone cold, then hot, then cold again. Was he saying what she thought he was saying? Was he going to ask her to marry him? Or did he just want them to live together?

She swallowed away the dryness in her throat and tried to force her brain to be calm. She took one breath. Another one. OK. OK. It had to be marriage. Whether or not they lived together couldn't possibly affect the rest of his life . . . could it? No. It had to be marriage. And if it was, it meant that he was saying that he loved her? Or was he the kind of man who could marry without love if the sex was good?

"Do you understand what I mean?"

And Lola looked up at him with solid black eyes that hid the turmoil behind them. For the first time in her life, she hadn't a single solitary clue about what he really meant. Was it marriage? Was it living together? Was it something else entirely? God. She couldn't sit still. She just couldn't. She had to know now. She had to know right this very minute. He couldn't do this to her for two whole weeks.

"Tell me now . . . Ask me now, whatever it is."

He bent, kissed her again. "This time, Lola love, you're just going to have to wait. No," he said as she drew breath again to object. "Not until we get back."

And she had to be content with that.

Chapter Thirty-one

The remainder of the two-week getaway was delicious torture for Lola. Every night, once everyone had gone to bed, Chaz opened the connecting door between their rooms and he spent the rest of the night with Lola's legs wrapped tightly around him. There were some nights when he loved her in a soft and tender manner, others when he was firm, demanding, passionate, insatiable. It was almost as though he feared that these brief days spent in Bermuda might be the last they ever had together.

After nights like these, Lola held him close with trembling fingers and prayed. Because although he didn't know it, once they did return to the States, one way or another, things were going to change between them.

Friday rolled into Monday and Monday into the following Sunday. And Lola threw herself wholeheartedly into every activity. They went snorkeling off Mangrove Bay and spent countless hours splashing around in the water and marveling at the beauty of the unspoiled coral reef. They went fishing for flounder during low tide and exhausted an entire roll of film photographing Jamie as he danced about on the beach completely covered in sand but holding up the first fish he'd ever caught. They even took a cruise ship out one afternoon to have a look at a sunken Spanish galleon.

Every evening, they all sat together at one of the dining tables and feasted sumptuously on fragrant dishes of poached crab, sweet lobster done the Bermudan way, wahoo steaks, black-eyed peas, and rice, and washed everything down with cold glasses of bittersweet Mauby.

The two weeks went by almost too quickly, and on the final day as she repacked her bag, Lola sat on the edge of her bed with her hand cupped under her chin, her eyes thoughtful. She had rehearsed over and over again in her mind how exactly she was going to tell Chaz who she was and why she had done this really juvenile thing. She planned to tell him as soon as they got back to the house. She wouldn't give him a chance to ask her that question of his, whatever it was. She would just sit him down, look him directly in the eye, and tell him. And then, if he still wanted to ask her his mysterious question, she would let him. Although she had the strange suspicion that after her little revelation, he'd be running like a pack of hounds from the property.

She kept that mind-set all the way through the trip back to the airport and the flight out to Maryland. It was only as they all huddled back into Chaz's truck and headed again for home that her resolve began to slip by just a fraction.

Chapter Thirty-two

"Well, we're home," Lola said, and she turned to give Chaz a speaking look.

He smiled at her and then with a frown of puzzlement rippling his brow said, "Looks like someone else is here, too."

"Someone else?" Lola craned her neck to see, and her heart shuddered in her chest as she caught sight of the little Toyota. A frown settled in her eyes. Damn it. Not now. Her eyes flashed to Chaz's face, and she could tell by the hard set of his jaw that he knew exactly who it was, too.

"Jamie, go into the house with Mrs. Lewis," he said once he'd brought the truck to a complete halt. "Let me handle this," he said to Lola, whose eyes were already spitting fire.

Lola climbed from the truck, slammed the door behind her. She knew exactly why the woman had come and only had herself to blame for waiting this long to tell him. But she was ready now.

Audrey stepped out of her car, gave Lola a hard little look, and then called out a breezy, "Chaz sweetie, it's so good to see you!"

Lola put a hand on Chaz's hand. "There's something I've got to tell you."

But before she could say any more, Audrey was upon them.

"I'm back from Los Angeles, and I thought we should have a little . . . talk." Her glance flickered over Lola, who was eyeing her like a pit bull might a piece of steak.

Chaz wrapped a hand about Lola's middle, pulled her close.

"We have nothing more to say to each other, so if you've come out here to start some—"

"Oh, I think you'll want to hear this." She tinkled a little laugh that had Lola itching to slap the smug grin off her face.

Chaz let out a tight breath. "What did you want to tell me that you couldn't do on the phone?"

Lola's eyes were like smooth black stones, and the expression in them caused the other woman to hesitate for just an instant.

"What she's trying to say, honey," Lola said, looking directly at Chaz, her eyes willing him to understand, ". . . is I haven't been completely truthful with you about my past."

"That's exactly right," Audrey said with a hint of malice in her voice. "And that's not the only—"

Lola cast a look in the other woman's direction and then cut right across her with, "I was hoping to tell you this in a different way, but, Chaz . . . I'm Sadie Green." There. She had said it. She had said the words that had been so very difficult for her to express all this time. And now he either would understand why it was she had done what she had done or would hate her for it.

She met his eyes with an unflinching look of her own.

Chaz looked from Lola to Audrey and then back again to Lola.

"What?" he said in a bald manner. "You're what?"

The palms of Lola's hands went ice-cold. So, this was it then. This was how everything was going to end, out here in the driveway with Audrey Mackenzie as a witness to it all.

Lola sucked in a tight breath and drew on that inner core of strength that never failed to come to her assistance in a crisis. Well, her story was *not* going to end that way.

"The fat little girl from high school. You remember her?"

"Sadie Green? You? You're saying that you, Lola St. James, are Sadie Green. That's what you're trying to tell me?" And, to Lola's amazement, he threw back his head and began to laugh.

Lola pursed her lips. Well, he was taking it all surprisingly well.

"That's right. Her name really is Sadie Green," Audrey chimed in now. She had played this very moment over and over in her head, but this wasn't the way she had seen it turning out.

"What're you laughing at?" Lola asked now, a tinge of annoyance beginning to creep into her voice. As far as she could see, there was nothing at all amusing about what she had just said.

Chaz wiped the corner of an eye. "Lola," he said finally, "I appreciate the gesture. Only *you* really understand how much I wish I could have a chance to go back to the past. Make amends. But you can't be Sadie Green for me, honey. There are some things in life that even you have to just let go." There was sincerity shining in his eyes now.

"But she is Sadie Green," Audrey piped in now, and she made a last-ditch effort to recapture her grand attempt at revenge. "And she paid me, too."

Lola's heart went as cold as a stone and her eyes flashed from Chaz to Audrey and then back to Chaz.

The humor vanished from his face. "Paid you?"

"Yes, that's right," Audrey agreed with a touch of smugness in her voice. "Seventy-two thousand dollars."

Chaz's eyebrows moved upward by just a fraction.

"Seventy-two thousand? Is that all you think you're worth?" Then he lifted a hand and said, "Don't answer that. Just go before you embarrass yourself even further."

Audrey's mouth went tight. "I . . . I . . . You just wait until she's through with you. I did some research on her, and let me tell you, she's done some things that—"

Chaz gave her a cold look. "Yes?"

"Oh, just forget it," Audrey snapped. "But if you think she's going to take you in here permanently so you can live up here in all of this, you'll see. Once she's finished with you, you'll be out on your . . . " and she laughed in a nasty manner and slammed back into her car.

Chaz watched her go. "And to think she was the woman I thought I was going to marry. My God. I must have been out of my mind."

Lola looked at the retreating car. "Chaz," she said now in a quiet little voice. "Did you ever take any pictures with Sadie?"

Chaz wrapped an arm about her shoulders. "Forget

about Sadie," he said. "I've something I want to ask you."

"I have something to show you first," she said. And she took him by the hand and led him into the house and up to her suite. He sat on the edge of her bed as she went back into a closet and rummaged around for a minute. She reemerged with a thick leather-bound volume in her hands.

"Remember this?" And she came to sit right beside him.

He took the album from her and turned it over in his hands.

"How'd you get this?"

Lola flipped the first page open. "You gave it to me, don't you remember? At the end of our junior year? You bought it for me one day on our way home from school. At old Mr.—"

"Chung's," he finished for her. "Jesus."

She looked up at him and the expression in his eyes made her swallow hard.

She opened the album, turned the first page, touched the shining plastic with the tip of a fingernail.

"Remember this one?"

"Jesus," Chaz said again, and he turned her face toward him with gentle fingers. He touched her nose, cheekbones, lips, chin.

"It can't be you, Sadie," he said in a half whisper.

Lola took his palm and rubbed it against the curve of her face.

"But it *is* me. I just look a little different now on the outside."

Chaz put her at arm's length and then hugged her

close again. Lola wrapped her arms about him in return, and they held on to each other for countless minutes.

"There are so many things I need to say to you," he began after a long stretch of silence. "I've wanted to apologize for so many years for all of those things I said to you. For how I just up and left."

"Yes," Lola agreed with a little wobble in her voice. "You said I wasn't a flashy girl."

Chaz pulled her close again and rocked her gently. "You know I didn't mean it. I just said that to you so that you would let me go."

"Hmm," Lola agreed. "Well, I'll make you pay for it. Don't you worry." And she snuggled closer to him. "So, what was that question you wanted to ask me anyway?"

Chaz wiped a hand across his face. "Now? You want me to ask you now? After all of this?"

Lola slapped him on the behind. "Right now, mister."

Chaz chuckled. "Do you always get what you want? Jeez. I should've run the other way that day I crashed into you and sent your books flying."

He reached into his top pocket for a velvety little bag that said "Bermuda" in fancy gold lettering.

Lola stuck out her left hand. "Come on. Come on."

Chaz removed the beautifully cut diamond solitaire from the bag and placed it on her ring finger. "You knew this was going to happen all along, didn't you?"

Lola beamed at him and lied her head off. "I did."

He pressed a warm kiss to her lips. "So, you will marry me then, Lola, Sadie, or whatever your name is?"

Lola gave him a pert little look. "Are you kidding me?"

Chaz hugged her close and rasped a husky, "Thank

God." Then, with a playful note in his voice, "You're not keeping anything else from me, are you?"

Lola pressed a kiss to the side of his mouth. "Not a thing."

And as he bent to kiss her again, she knew that she would just have to tell him about the bank loan and all the other stuff, later. . . .

Look for Camille's wedding in *She's Gotta Have It!*
Book #4 in the Champagne Series